The
Hedgehog

Zakaria Tamer

The Hedgehog

A MODERN ARABIC NOVELLA

Translated by
Brian O'Rourke

and SHORT STORIES

Translated by
Denys Johnson-Davies

The American University in Cairo Press
Cairo   New York

First published in 2009 by
The American University in Cairo Press
113 Sharia Kasr el Aini, Cairo, Egypt
420 Fifth Avenue, New York, NY 10018
www.aucpress.com

Dar el Kutub No. 16766/08
ISBN 978 977 416 255 8

Dar el Kutub Cataloging-in-Publication Data

Tamer, Zakaria
        The Hedgehog / Zakaria Tamer; translated by Brian O'Rourke and
    Denys Johnson-Davies.—Cairo: The American University in Cairo Press, 2008
            p.   cm.
        ISBN 977 416 255 2
        1. Arabic fiction   I. O'Rourke, Brian (trans.)
        II. Johnson-Davies, Denys (jt. trans.)   III. Title
        892.73

1 2 3 4 5 6 7 8   14 13 12 11 10 09

Designed by Mervat Waheeb
Printed in Egypt

Contents

Brian O'Rourke thanks Ahmad Karout, Bayita Garoffolo, and Wael Sawah for their help.

The Hedgehog

My Invisible Friend

My mother went to visit our neighbor, Umm Bahaa, but refused to take me with her, on the pretext that women visit women and men visit men. So she left me alone, promising not to be gone more than a few minutes.

I told my cat I was going to strangle her, but she paid no attention and continued grooming herself with her tongue.

I told the bitter orange tree standing in its bed of dirt in the courtyard of our house that I was going to get an ax and cut it down, but its leaves did not turn yellow in terror.

I told the wall that I would knock it down with a bash of my head, but it scoffed at my threat and dared me defiantly, "Go ahead, try it! You'll split your skull and be sorry."

Then I thought I heard someone moving in the upstairs rooms. I told myself, hoping it was true, that it must be an open window swinging in the wind, but I realized that not enough wind was stirring at that moment to disturb the smallest leaf of a tree. So I called out, in a harsh, long shout, looking up from where I stood in the courtyard, "Who's there?"

3

I was surprised by cheerful laughter near me. I looked around but didn't see anyone. "Who's laughing?" I asked.

I heard a girl's voice say, "I'm laughing. Is laughing prohibited?"

I said, "Who are you?"

The voice said, "I'm the genie of the house."

I said, "I don't see you. Where are you?"

The genie said, "Near you. You can't see me, but I see you."

I said to the genie, "What do you want from me?"

The genie said, "I don't want anything from you, but my mother went to visit one of her friends, leaving me alone in the house, and I'm bored and frightened."

I was astonished and said, "What? You have a mother?"

The genie said, "I have a mother and a father and an older brother who goes off to school every morning."

I said, "There are schools for genies?"

The genie said, "And universities, too."

I said, "How old are you?"

The genie said, "Five years old."

I said, "I'm a year older than you."

She said, "Don't lie."

I said, "I'm two months and three days older than you."

The genie said, "When I get bigger and become a young lady, you will be able to see me, as I see you now."

I said, "Where do you live? Where does your family live?"

The genie said, "Here, in this house. My father and mother sleep in one room, my brother in another, and I in another."

I said, "But our entire house has only three bedrooms, a guestroom, and a sitting room."

The genie said, "Your house is our house, and its rooms are our rooms."

I said, "Where do you sleep?"

The genie said, shyly, "In your room."

I said, "What color is your hair?"

The genie said, "I have long black hair, brown skin, and big green eyes."

I said, flustered, "I really like green eyes."

The genie laughed gaily and told me, "When you grow up, you'll like green eyes and blue eyes and black eyes and gray eyes."

I said, "I won't grow up!"

She said, "Yes you will, and so will I."

When my mother came home, she found me sitting alone on the floor, talking and laughing, and said, "God protect your mind! Have you gone crazy and started talking to yourself?" I told her that I was entertaining myself talking to a genie girl who was about my age. My mother answered in a dry voice, "You be quiet. There are no genies in our house. We only moved in here after your father brought in Koran reciters and a chorus of singers."

My mother wasn't interested in what I had to say about my friend the young genie, and she took me to the house of our neighbor, Umm Bahaa, imploring her, "Help me, Umm Bahaa! After God, I have no one but you! May God punish me! I shouldn't have left him alone in the house."

Umm Bahaa calmed her down and said, "Don't despair of the compassion of God."

Umm Bahaa placed her hand on my head and recited verses from the Koran in an undulating voice, until I grew drowsy and fell asleep.

I heard Umm Bahaa tell my mother, reassuringly, "Let him sleep, and when he wakes up you will find him cured, God willing, and he won't remember a thing."

For the first time in my life I scoffed, secretly, at Umm Bahaa, for a friend does not forget a friend. Then I realized that I hadn't asked my friend the genie what her name was. I was sorry about that but couldn't find out, even though I tried to talk to her later on. I didn't know why she was upset and refused to talk to me.

But when I grow up, I will look for a girl with black hair, brown skin, and big green eyes.

In my room, I no longer slept in the middle of the bed, as I used to, but moved to the right side, leaving the left empty, so that anyone who wanted to sleep there could do so comfortably and might be tempted to return another night.

Sleep

I wander around the courtyard of our house, which is flooded in summer sunlight.

There are five trees in the courtyard, a bitter orange, a sweet lemon, a sour lemon, a citron, and a fifth tree that bears no fruit. I asked my father about it, and he answered curtly that it was simply a green tree, which was reason enough for it to remain there and to care for it.

I pressed my right ear against the trunk of the bitter orange tree and didn't hear its heart beating and throbbing. I told myself that the bitter orange tree was asleep and must be different from us. It was asleep, and its heart was asleep.

My tree is sleeping.

The water in the pipes is also asleep, and will awaken if I open the faucet that holds it prisoner. But I have been warned sternly not to play with the water.

My cat is asleep and will awaken and start meowing if I bring a piece of meat or cheese near its nose.

The walls are asleep. I speak to them, but they don't answer.

The earth is asleep. I walk on tiptoe so as not to awaken it.

I look toward the yellow-white sun, but my eyes can't stay on it. I look at the sky, blue, with its single, small white cloud. I watch the cloud for a long time. It is motionless, as if asleep, or nailed to the blue of the sky.

Only the sparrows are awake. They fly from tree to tree, without a sound. However, when the sun starts to set, they shake off their languor and begin to twitter, as if bidding farewell to the sun, or welcoming the approaching evening.

The wind is not asleep but is content to give only a feeble gust from time to time, fluttering the leaves of the trees, as if notifying them of its presence and that they should always fear its anger, which carries off many of their leaves. But the arrogant wind doesn't realize that it only takes the leaves that have turned yellow and died, and that the trees are glad to be rid of them.

Like the wind, I am neither asleep nor awake, but I yawn and go to get the rug my mother sometimes prays on. I spread it out in a part of the courtyard of our house that the sun doesn't reach and surrender myself to sleep, pitying the sparrows.

A New Tree in the Courtyard of Our House

I stood barefoot on the ground between the bitter orange tree and the lemon tree, wishing to become a tree myself, convinced that roots would sprout from the soles of my feet and penetrate the ground. I held up my arms, which would become branches from which other branches would grow. My father and mother and brother will be amazed and puzzled and will ask one another about this new tree that has popped up by itself, without anyone planting or taking care of it, and without anyone noticing it. But, at the same time, they won't be able to enjoy it, because they will be sad over my mysterious disappearance and won't be able to find me, dead or alive. They won't be able to get me out of their minds, and it won't occur to them that I have turned into a tree with white bread, fresh and hot, growing from my branches. Whenever a loaf is picked, two more immediately sprout in its place, and no one goes hungry. Evil men who want people to be hungry attack me. Their axes swoop down on me, and I suffer and scream out in pain.

My mother heard my cry and came running out of the room, anxiously asking me what the matter was. I didn't say a word in reply, but kept standing in the dirt bed like a tree, without moving. Then my mother scolded me, "When are you going to stop this foolish performance? It frightens me."

She called out to my brother and told him in a mocking tone, "Your poor brother has gone mad."

My brother asked me what I was doing, but I didn't answer, because trees don't talk. I paid no attention to the mocking comments of my mother and brother. I continued to stand in the earthen bed, holding up my arms. I didn't leave it until my mother and brother sat down for lunch. I ate voraciously, for trees, too, die if they don't get adequate nutrition.

News from the Wall

I asked my best friend, the black stone wall, for the latest news of our house, and it told me that all was calm, that there was nothing worth mentioning. I said, "But since morning mother has been frowning."

The wall said, "If the walls of your mother and father's room aren't lying, the sole reason for your mother's frown is a disagreement she had with your father."

I said, "Why did Mother disagree with Father?"

The wall said, "Your father proposed moving to a new neighborhood and a new house, and your mother immediately rejected the idea. She said that she loves this house and won't leave it."

I said, "But if we move to a new house, you won't be able to move with us."

The wall said to me, scoffing, "Don't worry. I'll put in a good word for you with the new walls. They'll talk to you and entertain you."

I put an affectionate hand on the wall and said, "But the other walls won't be like you and won't fill your place."

The wall said, "Stop touching me, or I'll cry, and it's shameful for walls to cry."

So I left the wall and hurried to my mother and said to her, imploringly, "Is it true that we're going to move to a new house?"

My mother said, "Won't you ever get over your habit of spying and eavesdropping on others' conversations?"

I said, "Is the news true or not?"

My mother said, "Your father wants to move to a modern house, to an apartment in a building. He says he feels sorry for me and is fed up with old houses with courtyards that have to be cleaned every day."

I said, "But Father doesn't help you clean the courtyard. I'm the one who helps you every day."

My mother laughed and said to me, "If only you didn't help me! I can clean the courtyard in an hour. When you help, it takes two hours."

I said, "I won't leave this house."

My mother said, "Don't worry. We won't leave this house. I'll discuss it with your father tonight, and he'll agree with me."

I was about to ask my mother why she always chose the night for discussions with my father, but I contented myself with telling her, "I will tell Father that we love this house and don't want to move to a house that we don't know."

My mother said, "Children do not interfere in adult matters."

I said, "When will I be an adult?"

My mother said, "In twenty years."

I was annoyed and grumbled, "Humph!"

I held my tongue, thinking. Then my mother asked me, "What are you thinking about?"

I said, "When I'm twenty years older, will you be twenty years older, like me?"

My mother said, "I'll be twenty years older and an old woman."

I said, "Will you die when you grow old and become an old woman?"

My mother said, "Who knows? The young die and the old die. I might die a minute from now or in sixty years."

I said, "What will happen if you die?"

My mother said, "You will all cry over me for a few days, then you'll forget me, but I will continue to miss you."

I said, "I'll visit you two times every day, bringing a red rose."

My mother said, "Don't lie. Tell the truth. Will you visit me every day, or every year?"

I said, "I will visit you two times every day."

I imagined myself visiting my mother's grave, and rushed to my friend the wall and pressed my face against it. It said to me, "If you keep on crying, I'll be forced to cry even more than you, and a wall that cries becomes a laughingstock among walls."

I told the wall, "I'm not crying. My face is wet because I washed it, as I do every morning."

I imagined our house without my mother, father, and brother. The wall grew sad and became wet with tears, with no one to wipe them away.

Picking Bitter Oranges

I was rushing around the courtyard of our house, flooded in midday sun, imitating the bleating of a hungry and thirsty sheep. My father asked me to be quiet, so that my racket wouldn't awaken my mother, who was taking a brief nap after tiring herself out cooking, washing clothes, and cleaning house. So I quieted down and pointed with my right index finger to one of the branches of the bitter orange tree and begged my father to lift me up so that I could pick an orange that seemed beautiful and ruddy and ripe. My father was surprised and asked, "What will you do with it? These oranges are bitter and sour."

I said, "I'll examine it."

My father said, "If you only want to examine it, you don't need to pick it."

I threatened my father, "If you won't lift me up to the bitter orange tree, I will crow like a rooster and wake up Mother."

My father laughed and said, "Your mother doesn't mind the crowing of roosters, and if she wakes up, she might fix me a cup of coffee."

I threatened, "I will bray like a donkey!"

My father said, "There's no reason to be in a hurry. Wait until you grow up. Then you'll be able to pick what you want from tall trees, without asking anyone's help."

I said to my father, "I'm going to cry and wake Mother up from her nap and tell her that you hit me."

My father said, "Do whatever you like, but I suggest instead that you learn how to climb the bitter orange tree. You must master that, so you won't fall and split your skull."

I was upset with my father and bleated like a sheep and brayed like a donkey and cawed like a crow and croaked like a frog, and I cried and rubbed dirt in my hair, and my mother woke up. But my father ignored me, and I was forced to practice climbing high trees alone, taking care not to fall.

The Language of Fish

My mother was sitting in the courtyard of our house frowning, trying to darn some socks, when I begged her to tell me about the sea, which I had never seen. She told me in an exasperated voice, at the end of her patience, "Uuf! Aren't you fed up with talking about the sea? I've described it to you more than a million times, and my tongue is worn out."

I said, "This is the last time."

My mother said, "The sea is like a river, but bigger."

I was perplexed and said, "How can the sea be like a river? Isn't the water of the sea too salty to drink?"

My mother said, "Since you know everything about the sea, why do you ask me about it?"

I said, "Is the sea as big as our house?"

She said, "Bigger."

I said, "And do steamships the size of buildings sail on it?"

My mother didn't answer and her frown increased, so I asked her, "Is it true that some fish that live in the sea eat people?"

My mother said, impatiently, "And they'll eat you too if you don't be quiet and let me finish darning your brother's socks."

I said, "Do fish talk, like we talk?"

My mother said, "Fish talk, but no one has been able to figure out what language they use."

I thought about what my mother had said and then announced to her that when I grew up I would find out what language fish use, and learn it, and would persuade them not to eat people.

When my father returned from work in the evening, my mother told him what I was going to do when I grew up. He laughed merrily and told her, "But he won't be able to persuade people not to eat fish."

I glared furiously at my father, remembering him gluttonously devouring fish, fried or grilled.

Those Who Talk

When I meow like a cat, my mother makes fun of me. So does my father, saying that our house has two cats, a male and a female. My brother, who is ten years older than me and constantly boasts that he is studying French in school, also makes fun of me. I don't react to the teasing, but only smile, for they still don't know that I only meow when I want to talk to my white cat, whose language I know. I also know the language of walls, trees, and birds.

Cats don't say a word until they have given it long thought.

Walls are chatterboxes. When they are asked a question, they talk for hours trying to answer.

Trees like silence, with the rationale that talking saps their strength and makes them forget what they have to do.

Birds differ in their dispositions. A crow doesn't talk unless asked a question that arouses its curiosity. A dove likes gentle, pleasant talk. A nightingale's speech is all song. A common sparrow talks at a speed even faster than the speed with which it flits from branch to branch.

A few days ago, the wall told me that my brother has a magazine full of pictures of naked women that he hides under his mattress. The wall was not lying to me, for I found the magazine under the mattress and looked through it at my leisure. The wall asked my opinion of what I saw. I told it that my brother bought and paid for the magazine in order to see what I see for free when I'm at the public bath with my mother. I showed the pictures in the magazine to my cat. She yawned and said, "I prefer meat I can eat."

I asked the crow what the difference was between men and women. It thought for a long time, and then told me, "Women are afraid of crows; men aren't."

I didn't put the magazine back in its place under my brother's mattress, but hid it under my own mattress. For days my brother glanced at Mother with shame and obeyed all of her orders, thinking it was she who had discovered the magazine under his mattress and taken it. He did not get his magazine back until he gave me his blue rubber ball; it had been my dream to have a ball like it.

When I saw Mother absorbed in conversation with three women of the neighborhood, I went up to her and asked what the difference was between men and women. One of the neighbors laughed and said to my mother, "God's will be done! The next thing he'll ask is what the bridegroom does on his wedding night."

So I asked mother and the neighbors, "What does the bridegroom do on his wedding night?"

The neighbors' laughter increased, and Mother told me to be quiet and not interrupt grownups. She told me to go away and keep playing with my ball. That made me mad, and I threw the ball with all my strength. It flew high into the air, but didn't come down. I couldn't find it anywhere, even though I knocked on the doors of all the houses in the neighborhood asking about it.

After a while, I became convinced that a crow who wouldn't talk to me when I talked to him had snatched the ball as it flew through the air and given it to his son.

When I told my mother what had happened, she smiled and said, "Young crows have the right to play ball, too."

I did not agree with my mother's opinion. I continued throwing rocks at the crows, forcing them to caw in anger.

The Trap

My brother went into our reception room, and I tried to follow him, but he quickly locked the door from inside. I tried to look in through the window, but he rushed to draw the curtain over it. I hurried to the keyhole in the door and tried to look through it, but he blew snuff in my face. I started sneezing, one sneeze after another, and tears poured from my eyes. My mother, who was busy chopping vegetables, asked me what the matter was, so I told her what my brother had done. She laughed and advised me to stop meddling and sticking my nose into what didn't concern me.

Mother didn't notice my cat, who approached the platter of meat that she was going to cook with the vegetables, and ate every bit of it.

When mother finished chopping the vegetables, she stared flabbergasted at the empty meat platter and cried, "Where's the meat?"

I said, "The cat ate it."

She said, "Why didn't you stop her or tell me?"

I said, "I only meddle in what concerns me alone, and matters of the kitchen are not my business."

Mother cooked the vegetables without meat, and I ate them reluctantly.

A few days later, Mother didn't get angry when she caught me eavesdropping on my grandfather, who was telling my grandmother about his latest will and what it contained, and in an insistent whisper she asked me what I had heard.

The Delayed Gift

My grandfather coughed a few times, took a few swallows from the glass of water my grandmother got for him, then told her that his health was not what he would like it to be and that it was time for him to write his will, so that no one would be treated unjustly. My grandmother said to him, "It's a disgrace to think about such things. We have only one son, and the poor man does everything he can to make us happy."

Grandfather said, "And you? What will happen to you after I die?"

She said, laughing, "In my family, lives are short. I'll die before you and won't need anyone else."

Grandfather noticed me standing nearby and called me over and said, "Listen, my grandson. Your grandfather has been neglectful of what's due to you and wants to give you a special gift, but doesn't know what you would like."

I said to Grandfather, "Buy me a dog."

Grandmother said, "But don't you know that dogs hate cats, and cats hate dogs, and that there is an ancient feud between them?"

Grandfather said, "A dog would fight with your cat and might kill her."

I said to Grandfather, "Buy me a horse. I love horses."

Grandmother said, "What kind of love is that? Would you permit someone who loves you to ride on your back?"

My grandfather said to me, "Where would a horse sleep? In your room? A horse needs a stable."

I said to Grandfather, "Buy me a little television. I'll put it in my room near the bed."

Grandfather said, "Watching television will keep you from sleeping. You're young and need lots of sleep in order to grow up."

I said to Grandfather, "Buy me a bicycle."

Grandmother said, "God forbid! You will fall and break your bones."

Grandfather said, "And a car might hit you, and we'll be praying for your soul."

I was confused and kept quiet. Grandfather looked me over carefully and said, "The best gift for you is a comb for your hair. It is always a mess."

I looked at my grandfather's head, which had no hair at all, and said, "I'm the one who will buy you a comb; you'll like that."

Grandmother laughed, but Grandfather's scowl did not bode well. I was not given a dog who would bark at those who annoyed me, or a horse I could ride and gallop with through the fields, or a television to entertain me, or a bicycle that would make all the children of the neighborhood jealous, or a comb to comb my hair, which is always a mess.

Rose or Onion?

My mother saw me standing proudly in front of the mirror, with a cigarette between my lips. She snatched it angrily from my mouth and scolded me, "A sprout like you, smoking a cigarette? The cigarette is longer than you are tall."

I said, "Look at me. I'm a lot taller than a cigarette."

She said, "Who gave you the cigarette? Don't lie!"

I said, "I took it from Father's cigarette box."

She said, "Only one?"

I said, "One."

She said, "Don't lie."

I said, "I'm not lying. Search me."

She said, "When did you take it?"

I said, "Yesterday, after dinner."

Mother lectured me earnestly for a long time, and I put my head in her lap and fell asleep.

When my father returned from work that evening, and we were sitting around the table together as usual eating dinner, Mother told him what I had done. My brother laughed and whispered in my ear, maliciously predicting that I would get a beating, and advising me to be prepared or to flee. I looked at my father in fear, but his hand patted my hair, and he said to my mother, "This monkey of a child is certainly his father's son. When I smoked my first cigarette, I was younger than he is."

Mother shouted angrily, "Is this the way for a father to talk to his children? You'll ruin and frustrate all of my efforts to educate them."

Father said to my mother, as he continued to eat with gusto, "Come, come, my dear, don't make a mountain out of a molehill. A little rose grows into a big rose, and a little onion grows into a big onion. An onion doesn't turn into a rose, or a rose into an onion."

My mother's face grew redder, and she told my father in a menacing voice, "If you don't be quiet, I'll start screaming and walk away from this house barefoot."

I said to Mother, "If you start screaming, the neighbors will think someone in our family has died."

She said, "I will tell them that you died and I was relieved of you."

I said, "If you walk through the neighborhood barefoot, you'll hurt your feet."

My mother told me sharply, "You be silent."

I looked at my father, confused, and was about to say something, but he said to me, "Are you deaf? Didn't you hear what your mother said? You be silent and eat in silence. Not a word from you."

I didn't speak for the rest of the evening. I didn't respond to any question I was asked. I remained silent, and resolved to keep silent and not abandon my resolution the next day. Not a word passed my lips all day, and none of Mother's attempts to entice me to speak succeeded. However, I did inform my cat and the wall and the birds and the trees that I was on strike against speech. They weren't sad and didn't disapprove. They considered it the day of rest they had long awaited. This upset me, and I started insulting them all in a loud, disapproving voice. Mother came hurrying to me and said, "What's going on? I see that you've started talking again. Who were you swearing at? How many times have I told you not to talk that way?"

I said, "I wasn't swearing at anyone. I was swearing at myself because I upset you yesterday."

She hugged me affectionately, then got out a small camera and told me that the last time he visited us, Grandfather asked for a new picture of me. She made me stand in the sun, facing the camera, and told me not to move. She put a cigarette between my lips and took a picture of me, with the cigarette dangling from the side of my mouth, and told me, laughing, "I know your grandfather. He'll like the picture. It will make him laugh."

My mother took another picture of me holding Father's dagger, my right hand raising it high in the air as if about to strike. But my grandfather didn't get either of the pictures, because mother wasn't good at photography. In the first picture, my body appeared with the head cut off, and in the second there was nothing but my hand gripping the dagger with its curved blade.

Happy Days

The doctor was an emaciated man, with a yellowed face and yellowed fingers. My father had told him that my temperature had gone up and down a number of times during the night. The doctor examined me with slow, deliberate movements, and then asked me, in a hoarse and sleepy voice, to open my mouth. I didn't obey him, so my father said, "Open your mouth."

I opened my mouth as wide as I could, and the doctor looked into it with a small electric light. Then he walked to his desk and stood there writing. My mouth remained open until my father asked me to close it.

The doctor gave my father a prescription, and my father bought the medicine at a nearby pharmacy, in accordance with the prescription. We returned home, where my mother received us with a flood of questions. While my father and mother were busy talking, my brother whispered to me, "You poor fellow! You've reached the end. We will walk in your funeral procession and be rid of you."

I didn't respond, but stared at him in silence, despondently. My brother went to his room for a few minutes, then returned carrying a picture book. It was one I had always been curious about and had wanted to look at, but he never let me touch it.

My brother gave me the book, saying, "Enjoy it. You're not a child. You won't tear the pages."

I took the book from my brother and put it on my lap, without trying to open it or turn its pages.

My brother said to me, "You won't believe who I saw today. I saw the boy who tried to beat you up, and whom I beat up on your behalf, flattening him as if he were a sock. When he saw me, he was scared to death and ran away, because you're my brother."

My brother said to me, "When you've recovered, I'll take you to the movies, so we can watch the new Tarzan movie together. Lots of people say it's great, and very entertaining, and it's in color. Its star will come tomorrow, from Africa, to attend the first showing. What do you think of that?"

I said, "Will Cheetah the monkey also come to see the movie?"

My brother said, "I don't know, but Cheetah is bound to be there. I can't believe that Tarzan would come alone, without Cheetah. People would stone him."

I didn't say a word and closed my eyes. My brother said to me in a cheerful tone, "Open your eyes, quick, or you'll be sorry!"

I opened my eyes, and my brother offered me his two clenched fists and said, "Guess. In one of my hands there's something you'll like a lot. Go ahead, guess; we'll see if you're clever."

I chose the right hand, and, indeed, it held a beautiful little red car.

My brother said to me, "The car is for you, since you guessed the correct hand."

I took the car from my brother's hand and put it on the book.

My brother said to me, "In the school library today I memorized a story about the adventures of a man who grew so tall that the clouds floated by at his waist, and then became so short that he was smaller than a gnat. When he wants to grow tall, he grows tall, and when he wants to become short, he becomes short, as he chooses. Shall I tell you the story?"

Mother came in before I had accepted or refused, and gave my brother a spoon and a bottle of medicine, and said to him, "Help your brother take the medicine. One spoonful, and don't spill any on the floor."

My brother filled the spoon and brought it up to my mouth. I asked him, shuddering, "Does the medicine taste bad?"

My brother took a small sip of the medicine and said, "The medicine is bad; I'm telling you the truth."

I opened my mouth, and my brother emptied the contents of the spoon into it. The medicine was unbearably bad. My brother hurried to the kitchen and got a spoonful of fine white sugar and put it in my mouth, as if he were a nurse in a hospital. Then he said to me, "I'm going to the neighborhood market. Do you want me to buy some candy for you? Roasted peanuts? Cake?"

I didn't answer. I closed my eyes. I didn't hear the door of the house open or close. When I woke up, I found my brother still sitting near me, looking at me with bloodshot eyes, his fingers wringing a handkerchief nervously. I reached out my hand and took the handkerchief from him. Then I closed my eyes again, feeling as if I would get better without the doctor's medicine.

The Tattletale Cat

Before we went to sleep, my cat told me that my friends didn't like me. I told her that I didn't care about them.

My cat told me that all our neighbors were annoyed with me and hated me. I told her that all those who hated me would fall ill and regret it.

My cat told me that my father didn't love me, and only loved my brother. I told her that my father did love me and would love me even more when I grew up and became stronger and taller than my brother.

My cat told me that my brother didn't love me. I told her that my brother had beaten up all the kids in the neighborhood on my behalf.

My cat told me that she, and only she, loved me. I told her that was a clear lie.

My cat told me that my mother didn't love me either. I told her that was ridiculous. I yawned and turned my back to my cat and fell into a deep sleep. In my sleep I saw myself dressed in black, walking without fear among innumerable white tombs.

I Will Be Given a Sword

I was wandering around in our lane, obeying my mother's instructions not to stray far from the door of our house, when I saw the door of our neighbor, Umm Bahaa, across from our house, open suddenly. Her head emerged, covered by a large white scarf that hung down to her shoulders.

Umm Bahaa asked me what I was doing. I told her I wasn't doing anything, and that I hadn't found anybody in the lane to play with. She said to me, "Come see my husband's sword."

Umm Bahaa was a lively old woman to whom all the women of the neighborhood went with their problems. She lived alone in a big house with lots of rooms. Her husband, who had been an officer in the army, had died. She had no children, and I had never seen any of her relatives pay her a single visit. Whenever I saw her I would ask to see her husband's sword. She would agree once for every ten times she refused.

I entered Umm Bahaa's house, happy and amazed. She took my hand and led me into the reception room, where the sword was hanging on the wall. She pointed to it with her index finger, saying, "Here's the sword you like."

I tried to say something but was confused, and I stuttered and stammered. Umm Bahaa said to me in a mocking voice, "What's the matter with you? Have you swallowed your tongue? Speak!"

I wet my dry lips with my tongue and told her that I was tired of looking at the sword from a distance and begged her to let me hold it. She said, "Its blade is sharp and might cut you."

I assured her that I would hold it by the hilt and be very careful. She gave me the sword, and no sooner had I wrapped the fingers of my right hand around its hilt than I was struck by a sudden, mysterious force, mixed with pleasure, and started brandishing the sword, while Umm Bahaa cried out, "Calm down, you madman!"

I stopped brandishing the sword, and Umm Bahaa placed her hand on my head. She gathered a lock of my hair and examined it as my mother does, and asked me, "Is your hair blond or black?"

"Neither blond nor black," I told her. "Mother says it's dark brown."

Umm Bahaa kept feeling my hair and said, "What does she wash it with to make it so soft?"

I told her that Mother washed it with warm water and soap from Aleppo. I tightened my fingers around the hilt of the sword and imagined that I was attacking the kids of the neighborhood, unsheathing the sword, and they fled like panicked chickens. I smiled—a satisfied, gloating smile—and asked Umm Bahaa, "Will you sell this sword?"

She sighed and said, "The sword is precious and priceless to me. It's the sword of my departed husband. I look at it and remember him, and I wouldn't sell it for all the money in the world."

My face showed such sadness that it caused Umm Bahaa to laugh, and she put her hand on my shoulder and said, "I will not sell you this sword, but you will receive it from me as a gift when you grow up."

I said to her, standing on the tips of my toes, "I'm already grown up. Look at me!"

She said, "I will give you the sword the day you become a man with a mustache."

I asked Umm Bahaa what her husband used to do with the sword, and she said, "In the past, people used to kill one another with swords, in wars."

I said, "Did this sword kill people?"

She said, laughing, "If the deceased was telling the truth, it killed hundreds."

I touched the blade of the sword with my fingers and imagined crowds of men with the sword swooping down against their necks, and their heads flying into the air. I imagined that I was the one killing the men, and was filled with a strange, pleasurable fear I had not felt before.

Umm Bahaa led me from the reception room to the kitchen and gave me a big red apple. I refused to take it, telling her that mother had told me never to accept anything from anyone. Umm Bahaa said, "I will be angry if you don't take it. Your mother was only warning you about strangers."

So I told her I would take the apple, but only if she let me cut it with the sword. I ate the apple after cutting it in two with the sword. It had a strange taste, perhaps because the sword's blade had been stained in blood hundreds of times without being washed and cleaned.

Umm Bahaa died before I became a man with a mustache, and many of her heirs suddenly appeared. They sold the house and took all its furnishings. They also took my bloodstained sword.

I often saw Umm Bahaa in my sleep before I grew up. She was always wandering through her spacious house, with many rooms, opening the doors of the rooms and finding all of them empty.

Grandfather Talks
While Grandmother Sleeps

My mother and I went to the cemetery to visit the graves of her father and mother, which were next to one another.

I said to Mother, "Grandfather spoke to me just now and asked me to ask you not to cry."

Mother, wiping her eyes with a white handkerchief, said, "Keep quiet. Quit lying."

I said, "Grandfather says to tell you that I am not a liar and that you should not call me one."

My mother said, "And what else does he have to tell me?"

I said, "He says that tears are forbidden. They are permitted only when you are chopping onions."

Mother said, "And your grandmother? What does she say to you?"

I said, "Grandmother is sleeping. A sleeping person doesn't talk."

We left the cemetery and walked down the long road lined on both sides with trees and plants. Mother stopped suddenly and said, "I've lost the way. I don't know where our house is."

I said, "Don't be afraid. Take my hand. I know the way home and I'll take you there."

Mother laughed, took my hand, and we walked slowly along together.

When we reached home, I went into my brother's room and told him how Mother had forgotten the way home and I had guided her to it. He said, "You're an ass. Mother was making fun of you."

That made me mad, and I told him that I was going to tell Father that he smoked cigarettes in secret. My brother said, "But I detest cigarettes. I haven't smoked a single cigarette in my life."

I said, "I will lie and say that you smoke cigarettes, and Father will believe me."

My brother said, "Get out of my room, now, or I'll beat you."

I started calling out to Mother, and as soon as I saw her hurrying into the room, I threw myself to the floor and started crying. She bent down to me, asking with concern what the matter was. I told her that my brother had hit me, and he immediately denied it and accused me of being a liar. Mother paid no attention to him and scolded him, screaming, "How many times have I told you not to raise your hand against your brother?"

She picked me up from the floor, and took me out of the room. She washed my face with cold water, and I found myself crying, my eyes shedding real tears. I was surprised that I was not surprised by what had happened to me.

Eaters of Gazelles

My brother lost a lot of his self-importance during the days of his school exams and became kind, humble, and anxious. He promised me that if he passed the exams, he would give me a book full of colored pictures of gazelles. I said to him, "You will definitely pass, but you will forget to give me the book."

He swore that he would keep his promise.

My brother knew the depth of my love for gazelles. I had loved them since I saw a gazelle in the market tied to the door of a store that sells live chickens. I asked Mother about it, and she told me that it was for sale. I said, "What will the person who buys it do with it?"

Mother said, "Slaughter it, skin it, cook it, and eat it."

The gazelle standing at the door of the live chicken store

was beautiful. I had never seen such a mild creature. It moved slowly and watched what was around it with eyes full of a gentle sadness that entered one's heart and remained there and never left. At home, I would watch my brother, and whenever I found him with a cheerful expression and in a peaceful mood, I would assail him with questions about gazelles. He would tell me about them, as I listened humbly, as if I were in a mosque: The gazelle lives in the desert; the gazelle doesn't eat anything except plants; the gazelle doesn't harm anyone; the gazelle doesn't go to school every day; the gazelle doesn't travel by car but walks on its four legs throughout its life. I asked my brother, "How do people hunt gazelles?"

My brother said, "The gazelle is not strong and has no weapons to protect itself against people. As soon as it sees them, it runs, fleeing, and the gazelle can run like the wind."

I asked my brother, "Does the wind run?"

My brother threatened me crossly, "I will stop talking to you if you keep asking ridiculous questions."

I said to him in an imploring voice, "Don't stop. I will keep quiet."

My brother continued talking about gazelles and said, "In the past, the swift-running gazelle succeeded in fleeing and escaping from people, but they invented a car faster than the gazelle and began catching them easily."

I frowned angrily and asked my brother, "Who invented the car?"

My brother told me, laughing, "I, thank God, did not invent the car, and I didn't invent the airplane or the tank."

On the day the exam results were announced, my brother came home skipping joyfully, for his name was on the list of those who passed. I said to him, "Where's the book you promised me?"

My brother said, "What book?"

I said, "The book with pictures of gazelles."

My brother said, "I'll buy the book for you tomorrow."

I said, "Why don't you buy it today?"

My brother said, laughing, "It's not enough that you're a beggar; you also impose conditions."

My brother kept his promise. However, he didn't buy me the book, but a small ceramic figurine of a gazelle instead, claiming that all copies of the picture book were gone. I was not angry. I was delighted that gazelles had friends who loved them and wanted to know about them.

I loved the figurine of the gazelle. Every day I would sit near it for hours, looking at it and asking it lots of questions. It wouldn't answer, as if it were deaf.

One day I was playing with a ball in my room, and it hit the figurine of the gazelle and knocked it to the floor. It shattered and scattered in little pieces, as if a speeding car had run over it. I grieved so deeply that my brother promised to give me a live gazelle.

My grandfather and grandmother invited us for lunch, and we went. As we ate the rice and meat and vegetables, my father, mother, and brother outdid one another praising my grandmother's skill as a cook. So I told my grandmother that the meat was delicious, that I had never tasted anything like it. My grandfather laughed and told me that Grandmother's skill in cooking gazelle was beyond compare and that she was famous for it. My brother stared at me with a probing, questioning gaze. I pretended not to notice and continued to eat, as if I had no ears.

I Will Buy a Bank

My father bought a lottery ticket, assuring us that he knew in his heart that he was going to win the first prize when the lottery results were announced that night on a special television show. I asked him, "How much are you going to give me if you win?"

Father said, "I will divide my winnings into three parts: one for you, one for your brother, and one for your mother and me."

Mother asked me, "What will you do with your share?"

I said, "I'll buy a bank."

Mother said, "What will you do with the bank?"

I said, "I don't know."

Father sighed and said, "If I win tonight, the first thing I'm going to buy is a car, so I won't have to walk and wait for buses."

Mother said, "No, no, we don't want a car. Haven't you noticed that people have gotten to the point that they don't know how to be pedestrians? You might hit someone, and he might die, and you'll spend the rest of your life in prison."

Father said, "Then forget about the car. I'll buy a building."

Mother said, "Why a building? We have a house that serves our needs, and we don't need idle gossip. If you rent the building at a low rent, you'll lose money and people will think you have poor judgment and will mock you. If the rent is high, they'll say you're a thief."

Father said, "We'll buy a big television, with a screen the size of the wall."

Mother said, "God forbid! If a small television deprives you of sleep and only lets you sleep late at night, what will happen if we get a big television?"

Father said, "Why sleep if there's no work the next day?"

Mother said, "Even if you don't need to sleep because you won't be working the next day, I still need to sleep so that I can work from morning on—sweeping, cleaning, washing, and cooking—work that has no days off or vacations."

Father said, "You won't have to work at home either. I'll get you an army of maids."

Mother said, "Ugh! Imagine what exhausting work and responsibility when I have to supervise an army of maids and give them their orders."

Father said, "I'm at a loss. I'm going to buy a wide, comfortable bed. Whoever sleeps in it will get up only if forced to, and regretfully."

Mother smiled coyly and said, "I only like narrow beds."

In a little while, the lottery results were announced on the television, and father didn't win a thing. Mother was furious at losing a building, or a car, or an army of servants, and went to bed early.

A Lot of Dust

I saw an airplane tarry in the sky a few seconds, then disappear, and I told my father, "Some day, I'm going to learn to fly airplanes."

Father laughed, and said, "Since you drive us to distraction every day, I won't be surprised if you also start flying airplanes, without learning how."

I said to father, "An airplane is little. How does it have room for its pilot?"

Father said, "An airplane is as big as a house. There are seats and bathrooms in it."

I was quiet for a few moments, thinking, then I asked father, "How does an airplane fly?"

He said, "With gasoline."

I said, "Cars also run on gasoline. Why don't they fly?"

Father yelled out to Mother, pleading for deliverance from me. Mother rushed in and laughed when she saw our two scowling faces, and said to me, "Your father is tired and wants to rest. Today is the only day he doesn't work and can relax."

I looked at Father lying on the sofa. His eyes were closed and his face creased. I remembered a story my grandmother had told me one night, about a poor man who found a magic plate. He would cover it and make any wish he wanted, then lift the cover and find what he had wished for on the plate.

I would get ahold of that plate and ask for gold, which I would give to Father. Then he wouldn't go to work every morning, and would stay home and play with me and answer all my questions.

I would ask for gold and buy clothes for my mother that would make her more beautiful, and buy books for my brother, and fresh meat for my cat, which she would eat and be freed from her ravenous hunger. I would ask for gold and buy a bicycle.

Father stretched, yawned loudly, and got up from the sofa. Then he said to me, "Put on your shoes. I'll take you with me for a bit of a walk."

We left the house together and strolled under a blue sky and yellow sun, with the air of men who didn't have to do anything.

We came to a square full of commotion, with people crowding into it to look at a gallows surrounded by policemen. A hanged man was dangling from it. I asked Father about him, and he told me that he had killed an entire family—a man, a woman, and four children.

The hanged man's face was blue and his tongue was hanging out of his mouth and the people around him had cheerful faces. I closed my eyes.

In the course of our walk I saw a small child standing on the sidewalk crying, and no one asked him why he was crying. I closed my eyes.

On our walk I saw a girl faint. She was about ten years old and was taken off to the hospital without her schoolbag. I closed my eyes.

On our walk I saw a beggar woman sitting on the sidewalk with three small children whose faces were dirty and whose hands had been amputated. I closed my eyes.

I saw two men fighting, surrounded by people who were shouting at one another and urging the two to fight more fiercely. I closed my eyes.

Father asked me, "What's the matter my boy? Why do you keep closing your eyes, like an albino trying to look at the sun?"

I told my father that there was a lot of dust in the air, and I rubbed my eyes with both hands. Then I looked at them and saw that they were wet.

I took hold of my father's tough, strong hand, that would lead me home, even with my eyes closed.

The Suitcase

Four o'clock and my brother hadn't come home from school.

Five o'clock and my brother hadn't arrived.

Six o'clock and my brother hadn't come.

My father came home, but not my brother.

My mother told my father that my brother was late coming home, for no reason she knew of, and my father said to her, "Your son is a man; don't worry about him."

My cat returned from her evening walk in the neighborhood, but my brother didn't come.

Father said to Mother, "Your son is late."

Mother said, "Go out and ask about him."

Father said, "Where will I ask? At his school? The school locks its doors at four."

Mother said, "Ask at the hospitals."

Father said, "God forbid!"

Mother said, "Ask about him at the police stations."

Father said, "I have not set foot in a police station in my entire life, and I won't start now."

Mother said, "If you won't go, I will."

Father, angry and sarcastic, said, "As God wills. That's all we need."

Mother didn't say a word. She sat sullenly, as if she had turned into a stone statue.

At nine o'clock, the door of the house opened and my brother came in. He was pale, panting, and exhausted, as if he had been running for hours. Father glowered. Mother rushed to ask my brother why he was late, but he said, "First let me rest."

Father told mother sarcastically, "Didn't you hear what his excellency said? Get moving—bring him warm water for his feet, and a cup of coffee, and a cigarette, so that he can rest and in a few hours might feel up to talking."

Mother said to my brother impatiently, "Tell us where you've been."

My brother told us the reason for his delay.

He had left his school as usual, at three, and started walking home. On the way he noticed an old woman, over seventy, carrying what seemed to be a heavy suitcase.

The old woman would pick up the suitcase and take two steps, then put it down and rest, then pick up the suitcase, walk two steps, and put it down and rest. My brother took pity on her, remembering everything his teachers had told him about the need to help the aged. He went up to the old woman and offered to help her carry the suitcase. She thanked him, told him he was a fine boy, and gave him the suitcase. He picked it up and found it was very heavy. He was surprised that an old woman could carry such a heavy suitcase. He asked her where she was going, and she said she was going home.

My brother asked her where her home was, and she answered that it was very near.

My brother walked behind the old woman, carrying the suitcase. He would enter and leave neighborhoods, and whenever he asked the old woman about her house, she would answer that it was coming soon, that they would arrive in a minute or two at most.

The sun set, and darkness descended. My brother kept carrying the suitcase, walking behind the old woman.

My brother became weary. His pace slowed, and the old woman started to urge him along and scold him. He felt as if he were going to die of exhaustion. Suddenly he found himself throwing the suitcase to the ground and running away, followed by the screams of the old woman, calling him a bastard.

When my brother got away from the old woman, he realized that he was in neighborhoods he didn't know. He walked and asked, and walked and asked, until he arrived at a street he knew. He couldn't take a bus because he had forgotten his money at home.

When my brother finished his story, my father said, in a resigned tone, "There is no power and no strength save in God."

Mother said to my brother, "Dinner is ready; I'll bring it to you."

My brother said that he was tired and not hungry, and only wanted to sleep.

When I lay down in bed trying to sleep, my eyes remained wide open: After my brother's escape, the old woman bends over, picks up the heavy suitcase, and starts walking slowly. She realizes that she has lost her way home, but she doesn't stop walking. A six-year-old boy blocks her path. He is strong, with bulging muscles. He picks up the old woman and the suitcase, and delivers them to the home she had lost. She tries to thank him, but he hurries away from her. He runs back to his house, gets into his bed, closes his eyes, and sleeps. He is happy.

The Other Cave

My father, mother, and brother wasted an entire evening talking about the proper profession for my brother. Father admired lawyers and their ability to transform the guilty into innocent, and the innocent into guilty. Mother praised doctors and the speed with which they accumulated great wealth. My brother only wanted to be an engineer. I, on the other hand, preferred that he be a boxer, who could beat and humiliate the strongest men and make them cry. But no one paid any attention to my opinion. They finally agreed that the profession of engineer was not bad, for the era of tents had passed, never to return. The number of people was increasing, and they always needed more new houses. I elbowed Father. He looked at me, puzzled. I asked him, "What about me?"

He didn't understand what I meant, so I added, "Nobody asked me what I want to be when I grow up."

My father took my head in his hands and rocked it back and forth and said to me, "Before we ask you such a question, you must first be certain what's inside this head."

I said, "How can I find out what's inside it?"

Mother said to me, "Come on, speak up. What do you want to be when you grow up?"

I immediately answered, "I want to be a thief."

Mother was flabbergasted, and her eyes grew big. My brother flopped down on his back, kicking his legs in the air and laughing so hard that tears ran from his eyes. Father knit his brows and asked me in a serious tone, "From whom will you steal? Why will you steal?"

I said, "I'll steal from the poor and give what I steal to the rich so that everyone will become rich, and not a single poor person will be left."

My brother's laughter increased, and Mother asked me, "And where did you get this grand notion?"

I said, "Didn't Father get mad yesterday, talking to you about how many poor people there are and how few rich?"

Father laughed merrily and told me, "You'd better choose another profession. These days the poor are robbed of everything they have, and the rich end up with it, perfectly legally."

Mother said to Father, "Don't forget to inform your ingenious son that we are among the poor."

Father laughed and said, "What's the hurry?"

I went to sleep that night sad and ashamed, without reason, and in my sleep I saw myself moving along the trails of a towering mountain. I entered a cave full of gold, and the guard of the gold, whose voice I could hear but whom I couldn't see, told me that the gold was set aside for me and that no one else would get it. I woke up happy, but I didn't see that cave again. A few weeks later, however, when I was with my father and three of his friends on a hunting trip, I saw another, different cave. They said that a hyena that had devoured men, women, and children was hiding inside the cave. They lit enormous fires at the entrance to the cave, so that the hyena would be forced to come out, shrieking and trying to flee. They all opened fire on it simultaneously with their hunting rifles, but the victim wasn't a killer hyena, only a skinny stray dog.

Men's Secrets

My father ate breakfast, as he did every morning, but chewed unusually slowly.

When he finished his breakfast, he didn't get up in a hurry to dress and leave the house, but continued to sit, drinking glasses of tea, savoring them, as if it were Friday, but it wasn't. When Mother told him that he was late, he informed her that the textile factory where he worked was closed for the day for emergency repairs.

Father got dressed, whistling a happy tune, and Mother asked him, "What's up? Where are you going?"

Father told her that he was going to the coffeehouse, and Mother said, "Shame on you! You sit in the coffeehouse while I stay at home suffering and wearing myself out."

Father hugged Mother and said, "Don't be angry. You go to the coffeehouse. I'll stay at home."

Mother said, pointing to me, "Take that imp with you to the coffeehouse so that I can finish all my housework today."

I was delighted and seconded Mother's suggestion. I asked her for the clothes I would wear, but Father said to me, "Listen, son. I'll take you along, but on the condition that you don't tell me two minutes after we start that you're tired and want to go by taxi."

I promised him that I wouldn't get tired, even if we walked to the end of the earth. We left the house together and walked through the neighborhood, but Father didn't stop at the neighborhood coffeehouse. He kept walking. I pointed out this oversight, and he told me that he had agreed to meet some friends of his in another coffeehouse, not far away. As we walked along the busy street, Father saw me looking longingly at the window of a candy store, and he took me in and bought me a selection of the candies I like, and told me laughingly, "This is gasoline for the car, to keep it going."

I said, as I was devouring the candy, "What gasoline? What car?"

Father said to me, "Are you a donkey? Or are you just pretending?"

I was baffled and said, "What donkey? Who's pretending?"

He said, "Ask your mother. She complains about him night and day."

I said, "Mother doesn't like me. Whenever I ask her a question she says, 'Ask your father.'"

Father said, "What did you ask your mother?"

I said, "Yesterday I asked her why donkeys walk on four legs and we only walk on two? Wouldn't it be more comfortable if people walked on four?"

Father laughed and said, "Your mother was right when she advised me to gag you with a handkerchief so you wouldn't talk nonstop as we walked."

Father didn't gag me and, as we made our way down the street, he even bought me a shiny, colored paper bag full of chocolate balls, and he bought me roasted peanuts, and candies of various colors. We reached the coffeehouse before I finished eating what he had bought me. He had, in fact, arranged to meet five of his friends and colleagues from the factory. They sat drinking tea, and smoking cigarettes, and talking about the money-grubbing owner of the textile factory who resolutely refused to raise their wages. They had called a strike and stayed away from work. Father talked as if he was their leader. The other men talked, and Father talked, and the men talked, and Father talked. I put my face down on the wooden tabletop, listening to the noise of the coffeehouse, mixed with the rumbling of cars in the nearby street. Then I felt Father's hand shaking me, and he told me that I had been asleep for an hour or so. I denied it and said that I had only closed my eyes, and hadn't slept.

When we were walking through the streets headed home, I asked Father, "If the owner of the factory won't agree to raise your wages, will you continue your strike against him?"

Father was astonished. He stared at me in amazement and said, "You must not repeat a word of what you heard in the coffeehouse to your mother or your brother."

I remained silent, thinking, and Father said, "We won't say a word about the strike to your mother. She mustn't know about it. A woman's primary concern in life is that her husband work every day, so that no one in her family will go hungry. A woman is not like a man. She trembles at the slightest adversity."

Father was quiet for a few steps, then he asked me suddenly, "Are you a man or a girl?"

I said, "A man."

He said, "You're a man, and I'm a man. Men have their concerns and secrets, and women have their concerns and secrets."

Father threw his cigarette butt on the ground and crushed it with his shoe. Then he asked me, "Tell me the truth. Do you want your mother to be sad and to cry?"

I said, "No."

He said, "Do you want your mother to get sick and be taken to the hospital, where we'll see her only once a week?"

I said, "No."

Father said, "What you heard in the coffeehouse, and everything we said today, is a secret among us, the men, and the women must not learn about it."

I said, "My bother's a man? May I tell him?"

He said, "Your bother's a man, but he shouldn't learn about things that will get in the way of his studies at school."

I didn't say a word to my mother or brother, and for the rest of the week Father didn't go to work, on the pretext that the repairs at the factory hadn't yet been finished. One morning, however, he got up early, ate breakfast in a hurry, dressed in a hurry, and was eager to rush out of the house, in order not to be late for work.

At the door he said to Mother, winking at me and smiling, "Have you noticed that your son has gotten taller?"

Mother looked at me for a long time and then said to Father, "You must still be asleep. Your son is your son; he is neither taller nor shorter."

Father left, and I hurried to my parents' bedroom and looked into the long mirror. I saw there a man whose concerns and secrets were different from the concerns of women, and from their secrets.

Salt

Mother had almost finished cooking dinner when she realized that she had run out of salt. She reproached herself loudly and angrily, for Father was at the factory, my brother was at school, and if she went herself to buy the salt she needed, the food might burn while she was gone. She could find no solution to this dilemma but to send me to buy the salt from the grocer in the neighborhood market. She gave me money and accompanied me to the door, instructing me not to walk in the middle of the street, not to fight with any other child, and to buy salt, not sugar.

I walked quickly down our long lane, sticking close to the walls, and turned left into the street leading to the neighborhood market, with its produce, meat, grocery, barber, bean, and tobacco shops, and I saw three boys, older than me, who teased me whenever they saw me. I slowed down, despite myself, confused and uncertain, for if I returned home without the salt, mother would scold me, but the faces of the three boys showed that if I kept walking they would not be satisfied with teasing me in their usual manner.

I walked on as if I hadn't seen anyone, and as I approached, the boys laughed loudly among themselves. They put their heads together, whispering. Then the three of them formed a wall, blocking my way. One of them, the one with a brown face, little black eyes, and big ears, said to me, "It is forbidden to pass."

I said, "I'm going to the grocer."

The brown-skinned boy jabbed me hard and painfully with his elbow and said, irritated, "Hey! Are you deaf? Didn't you hear what we said?"

He turned to his two companions, asking, "What did we say?"

The two of them called out in unison, "It is forbidden to pass, and you can't do anything about it."

The brown-skinned boy said to me, "Did you hear? Anyone who wants to pass must do as we say and pay the price."

In my pants pocket, the fingers of my right hand clutched the money for the salt as the dark-skinned boy called out exultantly to his friends, "Look! Look at his neck! My God, how wide it is! How nice it is! Slaps can land on it like planes at an airport."

And the dark-skinned boy suddenly smacked the back of my neck with a hard and painful slap of his palm, and said to me, "It is now permitted to pass, in accordance with our laws, which don't let anyone pass for free."

I bent down and grabbed a solid rock from the ground, bigger than my fist, and fired it at the dark-skinned boy with my crazed hand. The rock shot out like a cannonball and hit its target. Red blood immediately gushed from his head, wetting his hair and flowing over his forehead, eyebrows, and eyes. The dark-skinned boy was scared, and sat on the ground crying and wailing in a voice like a woman's. His friends fled, and I ran back home. As soon as she saw me, Mother asked, "Where's the salt? Why is your face red, and why are you panting?"

I told her about my run-in with the three boys, expecting her to be proud of me, but she shrieked at me, blanching, "When will this nonsense end?! What will your father say when he hears about this? We are people who don't trouble anyone, and no one troubles us."

I said to her, "Don't be mad at me. Next time, to make you happy, I'll come home beaten up, with blood pouring from me."

Mother said to me, "What are you talking about? Next time? You can't walk alone in the neighborhood anymore, because the boys will be looking for you to get even."

But what she predicted did not happen. When I left the house and walked into the neighborhood, hiding a rock in my pocket, the boys were transformed. They received me as if I were older than them, and the beaten-up boy, with a bandaged head, was the first among the rivals to ingratiate himself with me.

I Asked

I asked the bitter orange tree that stands in the courtyard of the house how old it was. It answered that it was born before I was. And thirty years later I again asked it how old it was, and it told me, surprised, that men don't usually talk to trees, that children are the only ones who chat with trees and that they forget their prattle when they grow up. By then they regard trees merely as trees that bear fruit, or trees that remain green through all the seasons, or trees ready to be cut down.

As I was about to wash my face, I asked the water gushing from the faucet what it was saying with its rumbling. It answered sarcastically that, like me, it smoked cigarettes, was familiar with their serious damage to health, and was always pleased to mention the fact. I said, disapprovingly, "Do you dare to mock me?"

The water said, "Even if I am mocking you, what can you do about it, especially since I don't have a body you can beat, or a head you can cut off, or a mother you can insult?"

I swore not to talk to the water, for its character had changed. It had lost its kindness, delicacy, and refined manners, and had grown to love fighting and insulting people.

I asked the walls of the rooms what the latest news was, and they answered that television and radio stations were the only ones able to give the latest news, and that anyone who tries to compete with them fails.

I asked a cat if it remembered my beautiful white cat, who died after a sudden illness. The cat looked at me with disdain and didn't say a word.

The cemetery guard, with a drooping head and stooped back, saw me addressing the grave of my father and mother, reprimanding my brother who had moved away and hadn't replied to my letters for two years. He told me that the dead can't bear talk and prefer verses from the Koran.

I looked for my blue shirt and asked my wife about it. She said its collar was in tatters and that she had thrown it in the trash. I searched for my comfortable black shoes and asked my wife about them. She said they had holes in them and that she had thrown them in the trash. As I looked into her black eyes and tired white face, I longed to ask her about her love for me, but decided to remain silent.

I asked my young son what he was doing. He told me he was drawing a small village in which no one lived except cats and birds and trees. I stroked his head encouragingly with the palm of my hand and made up my mind to imitate him. I will draw a city without any living beings, and whose streets and houses are mountains of ash.

Short Stories

Summer

Her body was beautiful and warm. She tried to put it out of reach of his hands the moment he sat down beside her on the couch, but his arm had been quick to encircle her waist tightly. Her body was full and rounded and the softness of her flesh sent a convulsive shudder through his limbs. Though the girl's eyes were captivating, irresistible, they contained a pathetic appeal. With lowered gaze she said, "Let me go, Majid—please."

His face was near to hers. His lips approached hers and touched them lightly, just sufficiently for him to feel their delicate softness. At that moment he was overwhelmed by a strange sensation that almost brought him to his knees before her, letting his head drop into her lap, his breathing heavy.

"Let me go, Majid—please. I want to leave."

How could he let her go? Often he had implored her to visit him, and now here they were alone in a room with the door barred. How could he let her go?

"I love you, Itaf," he said in a low, trembling voice.

"You're lying," she said coyly, "You don't love me."

He was unable to define exactly the nature of his feelings for her: did he love her or did he merely desire her body?

He kissed her lips greedily and asked: "Why would I kiss you like this if I didn't love you?"

Though she knew the answer, though she saw it in his eyes, in the strange, hungry look that made her terrified, she was unable to answer his question. Some obscure thing within her body began to awaken, producing a hard core of alarm deep inside her. She wished she could close her eyes for a moment, then open them again suddenly and find herself in a street thronged with people or in her room with the sound of her mother's voice calling out from time to time.

She was unable to prevent a long sigh escaping from her lips as Majid's rough hand touched her body, a hand intoxicated by the smoothness.

"Let me go, Majid," she said. "Someone may see us."

"We're alone."

"The window's open."

A woman standing on the balcony of the building opposite laughed and said to a woman standing beside her: "Did you see what happened? Majid, our neighbors' son, has taken a girl into the house—his parent are away—and here he is closing the window of his room despite the heat."

Under the balcony a policeman's whistle blared out, followed by the screech of brakes as a car came to a sudden halt. A woman's face peered through the window enquiringly at the policeman.

The policeman stared back at the beautiful, radiant face. A moment of silence passed before he said: "You were speeding."

"I confess it," she answered in a sweet, gentle voice that stirred within him a mysterious tenderness.

A strange smile played in the policeman's eyes as he waved her on. The car drew away from him and he followed it with his gaze till it disappeared. The beautiful face, the voice, the smile, all these things had reminded him of the previous night when he had quarreled with his wife, of how he had got into bed and moved up close to her and she had not stirred. The bitch! She knew how to take her revenge on him, if he kept her short of funds, by presenting him with a cold, passive body.

The sun cast its flames above him; the street was deserted. He was seized by a strong yearning to be at him, stretched out in the coolness of his room with his wife beside him.

The sun was cruelly hot and the sweat poured clammily from his body. He stared at a girl who came out from the dark mouth of a building and made toward the nearby grocer's shop.

The grocer raised his head from his book of accounts and wiped away the sweat from his face with the palm of his hand. He stared at the servant girl who had entered and now stood before him. She was so close to him that had he leaned forward slightly his face would have been touching her breasts. They were so fully developed that he felt in awe of them. Many a time had he sought to laugh off this feeling of his and had tried to respond to her many advances, but each time the sensation of awe was too strong for him and he had been frozen in his tracks. Why was it that he always remembered her whenever his teeth bit into a ripe, juicy apple?

"What are you sitting there for like the dead?" shouted the servant. "Are you ill? Get up and give me what I want."

He continued staring at her for a moment, then stretched out an eager, trembling hand toward her massive breasts. Without moving the servant gave him a broad smile.

"Are you in a hurry?" he asked.

"They're waiting for me."

"Will you come this evening?"

She tossed her head and laughed softly, then stretched out her fingers and gave his lower lip a sharp pinch.

The sun blazed down crazily: the cool breeze was dead and the street semideserted.

Itaf rested her head on Majid's chest. "My father will kill me if he finds out," she said.

"Do you regret it?"

"No, I don't. When shall we get married, Majid?"

"We shall get married soon, my darling."

Majid took refuge in silence. Itaf got to her feet and said: "I'm going—I'm late."

Majid accompanied her to the door. Coldly he held her to him, kissed her. She was happy, her face radiant with joy. She kissed him passionately before closing the door behind her.

He went quickly back to his room and threw himself into a chair. He felt that the threads that bound him to life had suddenly been broken, leaving him at odds with everything around him.

Itaf's questions bore down into his very depths: When shall we get married?

He shied away from such a question. She had given herself to him and was now asking for the price: marriage. Everything in his city had its set price; no one gave anything for nothing. All were merchants of a new and superior type, lurking everywhere behind their various masks. How he loathed this type of human being! He loathed them savagely and now he had discovered that Itaf was one of them.

"When shall we get married?" she had asked him.

"We shall get married soon," he had replied at once, doltishly.

What was to be done? His mind refused to think about it. It had turned into a lump of solid stone. Depressed, he rose from the chair, put on his coat, and left the room to go out to the street.

The street was his great refuge. He walked slowly, heedless of the savagely scorching rays of the sun.

"When shall we get married?" Itaf had said.

"We shall get married soon," he had replied at once, doltishly.

Previously he had dreamed of marrying Itaf, but now everything had changed. If only she had yielded to him as evidence of her love! But that loathsome question had sprung forward brutally demanding its price of marriage. It had destroyed everything.

What was to be done? Majid came to a stop and leaned back against a garden wall. What was to be done? Should he marry her? Should he pay the price? There was nothing within him but disgust. He would not marry her—let tomorrow bring what scandals and calamities it might!

Majid spat savagely on the ground, then continued on his way with heavy tread. Before him the asphalt with its tired brown face panted under the hot sunlight.

Small Sun

Abu Fahd was returning home. He walked with slow steps, swaying slightly, through the narrow winding alleys that were lit by widely scattered lamps giving out a yellow light.

The silence that reigned all round him oppressed Abu Fahd, so he began to sing in a soft lilting voice, "Poor me, what a state I'm in!"

It was almost midnight. Abu Fahd's exultation increased, for he had drunk three glasses of arak. Again he burst out drunkenly, "Poor me, what a state I'm in!"

It seemed to him that his raucous voice was filed with an exquisite sweetness and he told himself aloud, "I'm in fine voice."

He imagined people with mouths agape waving their hands, cheering and clapping. He laughed for a long time, then titled his tarboosh slightly back. He resumed singing joyfully, "Poor me, what a state I'm in!"

He was wearing gray-colored baggy pants and had an old yellow belt around his waist. When he arrived under the arched bridge where the darkness was stronger than the light, he was surprised to see a small black sheep standing against the wall. He opened his mouth in amazement and said to himself, 'I'm not drunk. Look well, man, what do you see? It's a sheep. Where's its owner?'

He looked about him but found no one—the alley was utterly deserted. Then, staring at the sheep, he said to himself, 'Am I drunk?'

He gave a low laugh and said to himself, 'God is Munificent, He knows that Abu Fahd and Umm Fahd haven't eaten meat for a week.' Abu Fahd approached the sheep and tried to force it to move along by pushing it forward, but it refused to budge. Abu Fahd therefore seized it by its two small horns and tugged at then, but the sheep remained rigidly against the wall. Abu Fahd regarded it with fury, then said to it, "I'll carry you off—and your mother and father too."

Abu Fahd took the sheep and lifted it up and placed it on his back, holding its two front legs in his hands, then proceeded on his way while resuming his singing, his joyous elation much increased. After a while, though, he stopped singing for he was conscious that the sheep had grown in size and weight. All of a sudden he heard a voice saying, "Let me be."

Abu Fahd's forehead knotted into a frown and he said to himself, "May God curse drunkenness."

After some moments he heard the same voice saying, "Let me be, I'm not a sheep."

Abu Fahd shuddered and his terror impelled him to hold fast to the sheep. He came to a halt and the voice spoke again, "I'm the son of the King of the Djinn. Let me be and I'll give you anything you want."

Abu Fahd didn't reply but continued on his way with hasty steps.

"I'll give you seven jars filled with gold."

Abu Fahd imagined he heard the ring of pieces of gold

dropping down from some nearby place and striking the ground.

The sheep slipped from him, and he turned around just as he had been about to say, "Let's have them."

He found himself alone in the long narrow alley. He couldn't find the sheep and remained nailed to the spot for a while in terror, then continued hastily on his way. On arriving home he woke up his wife Umm Fahd and told her of what had happened.

"Go to sleep, you're drunk," she said.

"I only had three glasses."

"You get dizzy on a single glass."

Abu Fahd felt he'd been insulted, so he answered defiantly: "I don't get dizzy on a whole barrel of arak."

Umm Fahd uttered not a word and began bringing to mind the tales she'd heard as a child about the djinn and their sport.

Abu Fahd undressed, switched off the light and stretched out beside his wife, pulling the coverlet up to his chin.

Suddenly Umm Fahd said, "You should not have let it go before it'd given you the gold."

Abu Fahd did not answer and Umm Fahd continued with fervor: "Go tomorrow and take hold of it and don't let it go."

Abu Fahd gave a tired, sad yawn.

"And how shall I find it?" he asked wearily.

"For certain you'll find it under the bridge. Bring it home and we won't let it go till it gives us the money."

"I won't find it."

"The djinn live by day under the ground. When night comes they go up to the earth's surface and sport there till dawn draws near. If they have come to like a particular place, they continually return to it. You will find the sheep under the bridge."

Abu Fahd stretched out his hand to her bosom and thrust it between her breasts, where he left it motionless.

"We'll become rich," he said.

"We'll buy a house."

"A house with a garden."

"And we'll buy a radio."

"A large one."

"And a washing machine."

"A washing machine."

"We won't eat any more crushed wheat."

"We'll eat white bread."

Umm Fahd laughed like a child, while Abu Fahd continued, "I'll buy you a red dress."

"Just one dress?" whispered Umm Fahd in a tone of reproof.

"I'll buy you a hundred dresses."

Abu Fahd was silent for several moments, then enquired: "When will you give birth?"

"In three months."

"It'll be a boy."

"He'll not suffer as we did."

"He won't go hungry."

"His clothes will be beautiful and clean."

"He won't have to search around for work."

"He'll study at schools."

"The owner of the house won't ask him for rent."

"He'll be doctor when he grows up."

"I want him to be a lawyer."

"We'll ask him: Do you want to be a lawyer or a doctor?"

She clung to him tenderly and continued by enquiring in a sly tone, "And won't you marry again?"

"He gave her ear a light nip:

"Why should I marry? You're the best woman on earth."

They lapsed into silence, being immersed in a great, tranquil feeling of elation.

But after a while Abu Fahd took away the coverlet from his body with a sudden movement.

"What's wrong?" asked Umm Fahd.

"I'll go now."

"Where to?"

"I'll bring the sheep."

"Wait till tomorrow night. Sleep now."

He hurriedly left the bed, switched on the light that hung from the ceiling and began dressing.

"Maybe you won't find it."

"I'll find it."

"Be careful not to let it go," said Umm Fahd as she helped him wrap the yellow belt round his waist.

Abu Fahd felt that he was venturing upon some hazardous undertaking. He would be in need of his dagger, a dagger with embossed blade and swarthy gleam.

Leaving the house and setting off at speed till he arrived under the bridge, he was overcome by a sense of frustration when he didn't find the sheep. The alley was vacant, and the windows of the houses scattered along the two sides had their lights switched off.

Abu Fahd stood waiting, motionless, resting his back against the wall. After a while there came to his ears a noise that drew closer and presently there appeared a drunken man who was staggering and bumping against the walls of the alley, while he shouted in a drawn-out voice, "Hey, I'm a man."

On drawing near Abu Fahd, the man came to a stop and stared in utter astonishment.

"What are you doing here?" he said in a stumbling, joyful voice.

"Get out."

The drunken man knotted his brows in thought, then his face became radiant with joy, "By God, I too love women. Are you waiting for the husband to go to sleep and for the wife to open the door to you?"

Abu Fahd was annoyed; he felt his irritation growing within him as the drunken man continued what he had to say, "Is the woman beautiful?"

"What woman?" said Abu Fahd with exasperation.

"The woman you're waiting for."

"Get out."

"I'll be your partner."

Abu Fahd's anger grew more intense, for he feared that the sheep would not make an appearance because of the drunken man's presence.

"Get on your way or I'll break your head," he said fiercely.

The drunken man belched. "Are you ordering me about?" he said in a tone of surprise. "Who do you think you are?"

He was silent for a while, then added, "Come and break my head. Come on."

"Go away and leave me," said Abu Fahd. "I don't want to break your head."

"No, no," said the drunken man indignantly. "Come along and break my head."

He backed away slightly and said in a joyful voice, "I'll turn you into a sieve."

The drunken man plunged his hand into his trouser pocket and extracted from it a long-bladed razor. Abu Fahd put his hand to his felt, unsheathing his dagger, while the drunken man approached him warily yet with speed.

Abu Fahd raised his dagger high and brought it down, at which the drunken man moved to the left with lightning suddenness so that the dagger didn't touch him, and thrust the razor into Abu Fathd's chest as he shouted, "Take that!"

Withdrawing the razor from the flesh, the man backed away slightly. Abu Fahd clung closely to the mud wall and raised his dagger a second time, but the drunken man's razor again stabbed him in the chest. The third time he was stabbed in the right shoulder and at once his arm dangled limply and the fingers released the dagger, which fell to the ground.

Leaping about around him, the drunken man shouted, "Take this . . . . and this."

He stabbed him in the waist. Abu Fahd gave a moan and his knees went weak. He tried to remain standing steadily on his feet, but the razor was launching attacks at him, striking his flesh and tearing it without relaxation.

"Take that," shouted the drunken man.

He stabbed Abu Fahd in the stomach and his entrails spilled out. Abu Fahd pressed his hands against them: they were hot, wet, and quivering. He slipped and fell down. He lay sprawled on his back, while the drunken man, standing close by him, leaned over, coughed several times, vomited, then ran off.

Abu Fahd heard the sheep say to him, "Seven jars of gold."

Much gold fell down, glittering like a small sun. Then the sound of it began to move ever farther and farther away.

Death of a Dagger

Khudr Alwan was fed up with his mother telling him fantastic stories about new advances in cosmetic surgery. In a sarcastic voice he asked her, "And do you want to go back to being a young girl of twenty?"

His mother said to him, "Such operations do nothing for people like me, but they are of benefit to people like you. You can now get yourself a new ear in place of the one you cut off in your mad rashness."

Khudr looked at his mother crossly, at which she said to him, "You're now more than forty years old, so are you going to stay a bachelor your whole life? Who will marry you if you stay with just one ear? Every man in our quarter has two ears except for you."

Khudr said with confident pride, "And who told you I'm ashamed of my missing ear and that I don't boast about it?"

"Do you know," said his mother, "that the women of the quarter have forgotten your name and call you 'Lop-Ear'?"

"I'm a man," said Khudr, "and I don't care about what half-brained women say."

Antara ibn Shaddad, the legendary Arab hero who secretly accompanied him night and day, said, "Don't pay any attention to your mother's feeble-minded talk, for though my enemies used to insult me because of my black skin I remained the object of Abla's love and was held in awe by everybody."

"May God be pleased with you, Khudr. You don't understand a mother and a mother's heart. A mother whose son is a monkey sees him as the most beautiful gazelle. I want only the best for you and I see you as the most handsome man in the world, but take a look in the mirror to know that I'm not misleading you. You look awful. You neglect yourself as though you were an orphan; you shave off all the hair from your head and make yourself look bald; you let your mustache grow too large; you don't take care of your clothes, and you've got an ear missing."

"If you let your mother talk," Antara ibn Shaddad told him, "she'll be suggesting that you go to the women's coiffeur to have your hair done."

Khudr looked at his mother. He was sorry for her: she was in her sixties with the wrinkled face of a woman of ninety. She seldom laughed. Giving a sigh, she said, "Make me happy before I die, Khudr. I've become old and am at the edge of the grave, so when shall I become a grandmother and see your children?"

"How extraordinary!" said Khudr. "You have an army of grandchildren. My sister is married and has five little devils."

"But," said the mother, "they are the children of a stranger—they are not your children."

"Today's style is for men to imitate women and women men," Antara ibn Shaddad said to him. "Men have become scarce and their behavior is misunderstood."

The mother was surprised to see her son laughing, whose frowning face only moments before had been almost exploding with rage. In an impatient voice she said, "May God come to your aid with that twisted mind of yours."

Khudr Alwan left the house, after kissing his mother's hand,

and went to the Quweiq Lane café. He sat down on his own to smoke a narghile. Antara ibn Shaddad said to him, "Don't smile, for men when they smile too much become like flirtatious women."

So Khudr Alwan's face grew more sullen-looking, and the men sitting at nearby tables became convinced that a stormy dispute was about to erupt. They tried to distance themselves from him, but at that moment two policemen entered the café. One of them shouted a rough order to the customers to get to their feet and raise their arms. They then proceeded to search everybody one by one. On Khudr Alwan they found a dagger with a curved blade. Drawing it out of its scabbard, one of the policemen asked Khudr Alwan disapprovingly, "Don't you know it's forbidden to carry a weapon?"

Khudr Alwan mumbled a few vague incomprehensible words, at which the other policeman gave him a punch. "Don't speak through your nose like that," he told him. "The officer asked you a question, so answer it: Why are you carrying the dagger?"

"Because I like fruit," said Khudr.

"An excuse more vile than the offense."

"The doctor impressed on me," said Khudr, "that I should only eat fruit when it was peeled."

The two policemen laughed. They didn't arrest Khudr Alwan but contented themselves with confiscating the dagger and counseled him to eat fruit with its skin on, so as not to expose himself to trouble in future. Khudr sat in his chair aghast and abashed, as though he had been stripped naked. Antara ibn Shaddad said to him, "He who gives up his dagger is not a man and deserves to sit only among women."

"But it was a policeman who seized my dagger," said Khudr.

"Have you forgotten that policemen are human beings like you and me, that they die just as we do?"

Said Khudr to Antara, "Without a dagger I am weaker than a crippled old woman."

"And how will you get back your dagger?" said Antara.

Khudr sank into dejected thought, then all of a sudden rose from his chair and, almost at a run, left the café. He hurried off to the house of Najeeb al-Baqqar, the man in the quarter with the most wealth and the most influence. He met him and said in a quavering voice, "Listen, Najeeb Bey, all the people of the quarter, great and small, have come to you with demands and I am the only one who has not asked anything of you."

"That's right," said Najeeb, "and it's for that reason I censure you, thinking you don't like me."

"Today I've come to ask something of you," said Khudr, "so don't disappoint me."

"Ask what you want," said Najeeb, "and, God willing, your demand will be instantly granted."

In a choked voice Khudr related what had happened to him with the two policemen and asked him to get back his dagger, considering that the chief of police was his friend and would not refuse him anything. Najeeb thought for a while before saying to Khudr, "Why don't you buy yourself another dagger? I'll make you a present of the best of daggers, one that will cut through rock."

"I'd accept your gift with the greatest pleasure," said Khudr obstinately, "but I'll only be satisfied with my own dagger, which has accompanied me throughout my life."

"This very evening," said Najeeb, "I'll talk to the chief of police and everything will be settled just as you want."

On the morning of the following day Khudr Alwan hurried off to Najeeb al-Baqqar's house and found him still in his nightgown, stretching and yawning. He asked him eagerly, "Everything all right? Put my mind at rest, Bey."

In a voice full of regret Najeeb informed him that one of the policemen, instead of handing in the confiscated dagger to the station, had sold it to some foreign woman tourist and that he did not know either her name or her address. He was going to be severely punished and Najeeb advised Khudr to forget his dagger. "How can I forget it?" Khudr exclaimed. "Do you know that I haven't been parted from that dagger since I was ten years old, that at night I put it under my pillow when I sleep, and that when I go to prison the only thing that upsets me is not having it with me?"

Najeeb said to him, "Make a big thing of it and it becomes big. Make a small thing of it and it becomes small. Even the dearest friend dies, so regard your dagger as a friend who has died."

"I expected to hear such things from everyone else," said Khudr reproachfully, "but I didn't expect them from you, who are the great expert on the characters of men."

Khudr indignantly left the house of Najeeb al-Baqqar and walked through the quarter in an agitated state of mind. It seemed that his dagger was calling to him and he remembered how he used to tremble in rapture whenever he touched its blade and grasped hold of its hilt, convinced that were it to be hurled into the pit of a deep well it would of itself leap up to a mountain top. Antara ibn Shaddad said to him, "Were I to be given the choice between Abla and my sword, I wouldn't hesitate a single instant before choosing my sword, for a man without a weapon is a woman who will not escape being raped."

Khudr Alwan had the sensation of having become without any protection, a defenseless prey, and he yearned for an air different from the one he breathed. He left the quarter and walked slowly along a wide street, on both sides of which stood green trees and tall buildings of white stone. All of a sudden a speeding car ran into him and right over him. He was taken to a nearby hospital but died the following day at dawn. When he was breathing his last, Antara ibn Shaddad said to him, "You have lost nothing, so don't be sad; die unconcerned."

All the men of the Quweiq quarter walked in the funeral procession of Khudr Alwan, and at the head of it was Antara ibn Shaddad with bowed countenance. Khudr Alwan was proud of the fact that Antara had been part of the procession but was sorry that the inhabitants of his quarter did not know that and had not seen Antara piling up the earth with his sword over his dead friend.

Tigers on the Tenth Day

The jungles had journeyed far from the tiger imprisoned in his cage, yet he was unable to forget them. He would stare angrily at men who gathered round his cage, their eyes regarding him with curiosity and without fear.

One of them would talk to him, in a voice that was quiet and yet had a commanding ring about it, "If you really want to learn my profession, the profession of being a trainer, you must not for an instant forget that the stomach of your adversary is your first target, and you will see that the profession is both hard and easy at one and the same time.

"Look now at this tiger. He is a fierce and haughty tiger, exceedingly proud of his freedom, his strength, and his courage, but he will change and become as gentle, mild, and obedient as a small child. Watch what will occur between him who possesses food and him who does not, and learn."

The men promptly said they would be devoted students of animal training. Delighted, the trainer smiled, sarcastically asking the tiger, "And how is our dear guest?"

"Bring me what I eat," said the tiger, "for my mealtime has come."

With feigned surprise the trainer said, "Are you ordering me about when you are my prisoner? What an amusing tiger you are! You must realize that I am the only one here who has the right to issue orders."

"No one gives orders to tigers," said the tiger.

"But now you're not a tiger," said the trainer. "In the jungles you're a tiger, but now you're in a cage, you're just a slave who obeys orders and does what I want."

"I shan't be anyone's slave," said the tiger impetuously.

"You're compelled to obey me because it is I who possess the food," said the trainer.

"I don't want your food," said the tiger.

"Then go hungry as you wish," said the trainer, "for I shall not force you to do what you don't want to."

And, addressing his pupils, he added, "You will see how he will change, for a head held high does not gratify a hungry stomach."

The tiger went hungry and remembered sadly the days when he would rush about, as free as the wind, in pursuit of his prey.

On the second day the trainer and his pupils stood around the tiger's cage and the trainer said, "Aren't you hungry? You're for certain so hungry it's a pain and a torture to you. Say you're hungry and you'll get what meat you want."

The tiger remained silent, so the trainer said to him, "Do what I say and don't be stupid. Admit you're hungry and you'll eat your fill immediately."

"I'm hungry," said the tiger.

The trainer laughed and said to his pupils, "Here he is, he's fallen into a trap from which he won't escape."

He gave orders and the tiger got a lot of meat.

On the third day, the trainer said to the tiger, "If you want to have any food today, carry out what I ask of you."

"I shall not obey you," said the tiger.

"Don't be so hasty, for what I ask is very simple. You are now pacing up and down your cage; when I say to you, 'Stop,' you must stop."

"That's really a trivial request," said the tiger to himself, "and it's not worth my being stubborn and going hungry."

In a stern, commanding tone the trainer called out, "Stop."

The tiger immediately froze and the trainer said in a joyful voice, "Well done."

The tiger was pleased and ate greedily. Meanwhile, the trainer was saying to his pupils, "After some days he'll become a paper tiger."

On the fourth day the tiger said to the trainer, "I'm hungry, so ask of me to stand still."

The trainer said to his pupils, "He has now begun to like my orders."

Then, directing his words to the tiger, he said, "You won't eat today unless you imitate the mewing of a cat."

The tiger suppressed his anger and said to himself, "I'll amuse myself with imitating the mewing of a cat."

He imitated the mewing of a cat, but the trainer frowned and said disapprovingly, "Your imitation's no good. Do you count roaring as mewing?"

So the tiger again imitated the mewing of a cat, but the trainer continued to glower and said scornfully, "Shut up. Shut up. Your imitation is still no good. I shall leave you today to practice mewing and tomorrow I shall examine you. If you are successful you'll eat; if you're not successful you won't eat."

The trainer moved away from the tiger's cage, walking with slow steps and followed by his pupils who were whispering among themselves and laughing. The tiger called imploringly to the jungles, but they were far distant.

On the fifth day the trainer said to the tiger, "if you imitate the mewing of a cat you'll get a large piece of fresh meat."

The tiger imitated the mewing of a cat and the trainer clapped in applause and said joyfully, "You're great—you mew like a cat in February," and he threw him a large piece of meat.

On the sixth day the trainer no sooner came near the tiger than he quickly gave an imitation of a cat mewing. The trainer, however, remained silent, frowning.

"There, I've imitated a cat mewing," said the tiger.

"Imitate the braying of a donkey," said the trainer.

"I, the tiger who is feared by the animals of the jungles, imitate a donkey?" said the tiger indignantly. "I'd die rather than carry out what you ask."

The trainer moved away from the tiger's cage without uttering a word. On the seventh day he came toward the tiger's cage, with smiling face. "Don't you want to eat?" he said to the tiger.

"I want to eat," said the tiger.

Said the trainer, "The meat you'll eat has a price—bray like a donkey and you'll get food."

The tiger endeavored to remember the jungles but failed. With closed eyes he burst forth braying. "Your braying isn't a success," said the trainer, "but out of pity for you I'll give you a piece of meat."

On the eighth day the trainer said to the tiger, "I'll deliver a speech; when I've finished, you must clap in acclaim."

So the trainer began to deliver his speech. "Compatriots, we have previously on numerous occasions propounded our stand in relation to issues affecting our destiny, and this resolute and unequivocal stand will not change whatever hostile forces may conspire against us. With faith we shall triumph."

"I didn't understand what you said," said the tiger.

"It's for you to admire everything I say and to clap in acclaim," said the trainer.

"Forgive me," said the tiger. "I'm ignorant and illiterate. What you say is wonderful and I shall, as you would like, clap."

The tiger clapped and the trainer said, "I don't like hypocrisy and hypocrites—as a punishment you will today be deprived of food."

On the ninth day the trainer came along carrying a bundle of grass and threw it down to the tiger. "Eat," he said.

"What's this?" said the tiger. "I'm a carnivore."

"From today," said the trainer, "you'll eat nothing but grass."

When the tiger's hunger became unbearable he tried to eat the grass, but he was shocked by its taste and moved away from it in disgust. However, the tiger returned to it and very gradually began to find its taste pleasant.

On the tenth day the trainer, the pupils, the tiger, and the cage disappeared—the tiger became a citizen and the cage a city.

A Summary of What Happened
to Muhammad al-Mahmoudi

Muhammad al-Mahmoudi was an elderly man who
lived alone in a small house. He had neither wife nor
children and, being retired, had nothing to do. First
thing in the morning he would leave the house and walk leisurely through the streets, stopping for a few moments to buy
his favorite newspaper and then continuing his slow promenade
in the direction of a café separated from the noisy street by a
glass wall. On arrival he would go inside and make for a particular table which afforded him the opportunity of observing
the street; there he would sit waiting, without saying anything,
for the narghile and cup of sugarless coffee. Then, taking from
his pocket a pair of spectacles, he would put them on and would
become engrossed in reading the newspaper, smoking his narghile and looking out from time to time with bemused eyes at the
street.

When he felt hungry, he would rise with sluggish reluc-
tance and leave the café for a nearby restaurant. He would eat

listlessly, then quickly return to the café to carry on reading the newspaper, smoking his narghile, sipping tea and coffee, and watching the street until nightfall, at which time he would leave the café, go home, take off his clothes, lie down on his wide bed, and at once fall into a deep sleep.

Sometimes he would see his mother in his sleep. She would upbraid him severely for not having married and bewailingly demand a child who would say to her, "Granny, buy me a balloon."

So he would arise from sleep, dejected and embarrassed at his desire to weep loud and long.

One day he was sitting as usual at the café reading the newspaper and smoking his narghile when the newspaper suddenly slipped from his fingers and, with a moan, he collapsed to the ground. The doctor was immediately called and confidently pronounced that he was dead. Then, in fulfillment of his will, pickaxes and spades were brought and a hole was dug under the table at which he had been accustomed to sit, and he was gently taken up and laid to rest in the bottom of the hole and a lot of earth was heaped on top of him. He didn't grumble or get annoyed but smiled happily at being released from having to walk the streets and go to the house and the restaurant, and he listened ardently to the conversations of the café's clientele, the gurgling of the narghiles, and the shouts of the waiters. At night, though, he would feel bored, lonely, and frightened, for the café would be empty and its doors closed.

The day came when the café was raided by a number of policemen. They extracted Muhammad al-Mahmoudi from his hole and led him off to a police station. There the police superintendent said to him in a stern voice, "It has come to our knowledge that you criticize the acts of the government, make fun of it, curse it, and claim that all its laws serve only the owners of properties, cars, and large stomachs."

In terrified remonstration Muhammad al-Mahmoudi called out, "I curse the government? God forbid! I am not one of those who drink from a well and then spit into it. Ask about me. I was an exemplary official and I used to obey orders and laws and would carry them out meticulously. Ask about me. I never once got drunk, never made a pass at a woman, never harmed anyone, and I was . . . ."

The superintendent interrupted him, "But the reports that have come in to us about you don't lie and the people who made them are wholly trustworthy."

Muhammad al-Mahmoudi shuddered and said in a quaking voice, "I swear by God that I have lived my whole life without ever talking about politics, and never ever have I insulted the government or those in power."

"Ha ha," said the superintendent, "I condemn you out of your own mouth. You say you haven't insulted the government, but you don't say that you have praised it. Does it not in your opinion deserve praise?"

Muhammad al-Mahmoudi tried to speak, but the superintendent continued talking, "And even if what you say is true, it sounds most strange, for everyone else has become twisted, spiteful, and embittered. People insult the government and those in power, oblivious of the necessity to obey authority. They don't realize that it isn't everyone who understands politics."

Muhammad al-Mahmoudi said in a faint voice, "That's so. Everyone is talking about politics and ascribing the most disgraceful attributes to every single responsible person in the state. As for me . . . ."

Interrupting him with a meek questioning voice, the superintendent said, "And of course in the café you hear what they say and know the names of those speaking?"

Muhammad al-Mahmoudi nodded his head. The super-intendent smiled and said, "It would appear you are a good man and an upright citizen, and I would really like to help you in order that you may escape from the accusation leveled at you, but you too must help me."

Muhammad al-Mahmoudi said in astonishment, "And how am I to help you when I'm dead?"

The superintendent gave a cheerful laugh, then said, "It's very simple and interesting. Listen . . . "

Muhammad al-Mahmoudi listened to what the superintendent had to say, then after a while returned to his hole in the café in a very joyful state, for now he had something to do. No longer would he feel lonely, bored, and frightened when the café closed its doors at midnight: it was then that he would hasten to write down, lest he forget, the conversations of the café's clientele.

Sun for the Young

I said to my brother who was lying on the bed, "You're like a frog."

He said to me, "When you grow up you'll become a thief and I'll be a policeman and I'll arrest you and put you in prison."

I said him, "I'm not frightened of policemen."

He said, "That's how a thief talks."

I got annoyed and said to him, "I'll hit you in the face."

He screamed in a loud, shrill voice, and my mother came along from the kitchen. Putting a hand to his cheek and pointing with the other, my brother said to her, "He hit me in the face."

"Liar!" I shouted.

"Shut up you two," said my mother furiously.

Then she put her hand on my shoulder and said, "Go along and buy some milk."

"Send my brother," I said.

"Can't you see he's sick?" she said.

"I too am sick," I said.

"You're as fit as a flea," she said.

"My foot hurts," I said.

She didn't believe me, and I was forced to leave the house. The fingers of my right hand tightly clenched the money, while my left hand carefully held the bowl, for my mother had directed me not to lose the money, break the bowl, or spill the milk.

I walked slowly to the grocer's, where I found him sitting on a chair in front of the door of the shop. He was fat, with a stomach like that of a pregnant woman.

"Do you have any milk?" I said to him.

He yawned and chased away with his hand a fly that was about to enter his mouth. "Goats' milk or cows' milk?" he said.

I was taken by surprise by his question. "I don't know," I said.

"Go back and ask your mother," he said.

I returned home and told my mother of the grocer's question.

"Get cows' milk," she said angrily.

So I returned to the grocer's and said, "My mother wants cows' milk."

"There's only goats' milk," he said.

So I went home again and said to my mother, "There's only goats' milk."

She got even angrier and said, "Go and bring back goats' milk."

Returning to the grocer's, I said to him, "Give me goats' milk."

He took the money from me and counted it out with painstaking deliberateness, then threw it into an iron drinking vessel placed on a wooden shelf. Placing the bowl in the scale of the balance, he then put the milk into the bowl, which he gave me. He directed me not to spill the milk, so I went off with slow, cautious steps, my eyes glued to the milk that swayed in the bowl. Suddenly my way was blocked by a fair-complexioned boy, well dressed and with hair combed.

"You're a servant," he said to me scornfully.

"Your mother's a washerwoman and a beggar," I said to him in anger.

"My father's got a car," he said. "Has your father got a car?"

I didn't utter a word, so he approached me and stretched out his hand with the fingers clenched.

"Guess what I've got in my hand?" he asked me.

"I don't know," I said, my anger having abated.

"Go on, guess," he said.

"Five piasters," I said.

"No," he said, "you haven't guessed."

He opened his hand and there on the outstretched palm was a dead fly. "I caught it," he said proudly.

I felt disgusted and the boy laughed derisively and threw the dead fly into the bowl. I caught him and struck him with the bowl and the milk went all over his clothes, and the bowl fell to the ground and was shattered.

They boy sat on the ground and began howling and crying like a girl. The sight of him was funny, but I was frightened and ran off. I didn't come to a stop till I was tired, when I leaned against a mud wall, panting and at a loss, for my mother would hit me if I returned home without the bowl of milk and my brother would look at me and gloat over my misfortune.

The alley was empty, so I cried, then wiped away the tears with my sleeve and sat down on the ground, tired and not knowing what to do.

All at once I became aware of a ring lying close by me. I picked it up and it appeared to be of silver, though it wasn't clean. I began rubbing it against my clothes and, then and there, a black cat came toward me mewing. I drove it away, saying, "Get away!"

It mewed again and said to me, "What do you want?"

I was frightened, but I gathered courage, regained my breath with difficulty, then said to it, "Who are you?"

"I'm the demon, servant of the ring."

"You're a cat," I said to it.

"I come in disguise lest people be afraid of me," it said. "Come on, ask what you want and I'll grant your wish."

I thought for a while, then said to it, "I want a bowl of milk in place of the bowl that broke."

"Your wish will be fulfilled," it said. "Here's the bowl."

Joyfully I took up the bowl though I was a little upset to find a dead fly floating on the surface of the milk. However, with cheerful, confident step, I set off homeward.

Snow at the End of the Night

Yusuf pressed his forehead against the pane of the window that overlooked the street. The night outside the room was a cold black rose, as snow fell slowly across a space of sickly light. At that moment Yusuf's mother was putting the teapot on the stove. His father sat in silence, dejection showing on his wrinkled face, a secret discontent gleaming in his eyes; his hands lay inert on his knees like two tired, elderly friends.

It exasperated Yusuf when the cat again rubbed itself against his legs, and he kicked at in disgust.

The cat shrank back in pain and crouched down near the stove. It closed its eyes in defeat and began dreaming of having discovered a garden with very high walls, the ground covered with a layer of wingless birds; choosing a plump one, it would glare at it ravenously and the bird would cower in terror.

"I'm a poor little bird," it would say in a high-pitched, quavering voice.

"I'm hungry."

"I'll sing for you."

"I'm hungry."

The cat would pounce upon the little bird savagely and sink its small sharp teeth into its throat, tearing at its juicy throat till the blood ran warm and crimson.

Yusuf pressed his forehead against the cool glass as he formed in his mind the face of his sister who had run away—a gentle girl who was ever smiling. He said to himself, "I'll kill her when I find her. I'll sever her head from her body."

"Aren't you tired of standing?" he heard his father say to him.

Yusuf stood motionless and silent. His mother hastened to break in, "I forgot to tell you what I saw last night. I saw her!"

In surprise Yusuf turned round quickly. When his eyes met her face he realized at once that she had again seen the snake that lay hidden in their old, mud-walled house. Yusuf imagined the snake: black, smooth, sleek, sliding silently across the courtyard under the light of the moon that had come out yesterday.

"How beautiful she was! She was like a queen."

Yusuf felt that the snake was real, a wonderful queen whose slaves had all died while she remained living alone in a desolate land. An old anger awoke within him. Directing his words at his father, he said, "She'll harm us, we must do away with her."

A secret joy flickered in his father's eyes as he replied, "She harms only those who harm her. She has lived in the house since before you were born and has harmed no one."

Yusuf was convinced that the snake knew he hated her and was waiting for the moment to advance against him and bring about his destruction. He had many times asked his father that they should go to live in a new house built of iron, cement, and stone. Forming in his imagination would be white buildings, like delicate poems filled with a sun that never set, but his father would refuse, obstinately saying, "Here I was born and here I'll die."

Yusuf watched his father's face with resentment. His father

coughed, then continued sarcastically, "Find her if you can and kill her."

"I'll find her," Yusuf said to himself. "She'll not escape me." Yusuf peered malevolently at the empty seat close to the window. His sister was accustomed to sit there in the evenings, talking and laughing and playing with her cat. But where was she now?

Yusuf craved a cigarette. The cigarettes were in his pocket, but he didn't dare smoke in front of his father. He therefore made for the door and his father promptly enquired of him, "Where are you off to?"

"I'm tired and want to go to bed," said Yusuf.

"You poor thing," said his father, "you have so much work to do. Are you breaking stones all day? How can you get tired when you don't do anything? Does yawning tire you out? Tell me, haven't you found any work?"

His mother protested with the words, "He's ill. Look at him, look how thin and pale he is."

Yusuf sensed that the moment he feared was about to arrive.

"You're the one to blame," his father shouted angrily. "It's you who've spoilt the children—my young son eats and sleeps, my daughter runs away, my wife gossips with neighbors, while I work like a donkey."

"Don't shout so," pleaded the mother, "or the neighbors will hear."

"I'll shout as much as I please."

His father, lowering his head, went on in a doleful tone, "O God, what have I done that I should be disgraced at the end of my life?"

"Didn't I tell you," said the mother, "to inform the police of her disappearance?"

"You shouldn't have left her alone. If you hadn't left the house and gone off to the neighbors, she wouldn't have been able to make her escape. Why didn't you take her with you?"

"The poor thing was so tired after having cleaned the whole house."

"Poor thing! The poor thing deserves to have her throat cut. What are we going to say to our neighbors when they visit us and don't find her at home? Shall we say to them, 'Her mother was at the neighbors' so the girl took most of her clothes and ran away we don't know where'?"

The father turned to Yusuf. "I want you to search for her and find her whatever it takes," he said sternly. "Slit her throat for her, as you would a bitch."

Yusuf recollected the days of his childhood when the sheep were slaughtered outside the butchers' shops on feast days—the sheep letting out terrified cries as it lay, unable to free itself, under the butcher's weight. The butcher's sharp, large-bladed knife would penetrate the sheep's throat and the blood would spurt out of a deep red wound.

The mother burst into tears. "She's my own daughter," she cried out. "The two of you haven't given a thought for her or for me."

Opening the door, Yusuf slipped out. On closing the door behind him he felt a strange sense of peace and quickly lit a cigarette. Slowly he inhaled the smoke as he paced up and down his room with short restive steps, listening to the sound of his shoes on the stone floor. After a while, he came to a stop by a wooden table and contemplated it sadly, for here was where his small radio had stood, the one his father had made him sell.

The radio had been a faithful friend to Yusuf. Now, having parted with it, he was a young man without music. He felt the cold intensifying around him, so he undressed, switched off the light and buried himself under the bedcover, with his head resting on the pillow.

He was convinced that the snake must be hiding somewhere in the house or was quietly slithering through the rooms. He closed his eyes and his yearning for music grew and erupted within him like a cloud that has been transformed into a rainstorm on rough ground. He listened to the mysterious music that came from deep inside him, while he sobbed and left his tears unwiped.

Yusuf felt that he might, shortly, weep violently; that, at one and the same time, he was both the rain and the parched earth. He had the sensation that there was some unknown world, a world so close to him from which he was separated by no more than a bridge of glass. "I'm ill," he said to himself, "ill."

Yusuf darted forward and, swiftly traversing the glass bridge, was embraced by the compassion of a vast obscure world whose master was dense darkness. There formed in Yusuf's imagination the ruins of cities, their buildings razed. He cried out soundlessly, "My life is being squandered. I want another life, one without a father." The sadness stifled within him exploded: "The trees are green stars. My heart knocks against a closed door. My tears are the children of a senile sadness. For whom does the face of the sun pale? Night is a pillow that loves those who are weary. My blood drains from me, spilled by the absence of a woman whose breast sleeps on a blue rug, dreaming of cities of men."

Yusuf shivered under the bedcover, certain that he was ill. Hunting for stars, he said, "Would that the wound did not scream and say, 'Rise up, O sun of wrath.'" And death comes disguised in sailor's garb and Yusuf says to it, "Let your boat carry me across to the shore." The other shore was a green voice that called to Yusuf with great tenderness. But death did not answer; its boat sailed off and Yusuf waved to travelers with wan faces. The music-lovers came forward, bearing drums and trumpets, wandering through deserted gardens. The night was a woman's hair. No, the night was a snake slithering deeply into the heart of the world. One of the music-lovers groaned, then raised his trumpet to his mouth; the brass glistened for an instant, then gave out a long harsh blast. He cast aside shame and gave a wail that was like the sound of crushed humankind living in humiliation on the hard earth.

Yusuf was now a sword, a cloak fondled by the wind, a stallion galloping over desert sands. He heard a woman calling for help, "My sister's calling to me."

Yusuf wished the snake might come at that instant; he didn't want it to kill him with its poison but wished for its cold body to coil itself round his neck and for it to go on exerting pressure until he was choked and rendered motionless. Thus he would be far removed from his father and his mother and the knife thirsty for blood.

Yusuf licked his dry lips. He didn't wish to submit to sleep, for he knew that while he slept he would see seven lean cows lowing mournfully as they grazed in a field without grass, and that the sky would be a low, solid roof of locusts and flies.

Yusuf would not yield to despair. He would continue to look for his sister throughout the winter day, roaming about under the rain and the snow, heedless of the wind and the frost. But, unable to find her, he would gaze sadly at the bare trees that would be like beggar women, while his fingers would not let go of the handle of the knife that lay in his pocket.

He recalled to mind the day his sister had asked permission of his father to go to the cinema with her cousins, the daughters of her maternal aunt, and he had slapped her hard. Yusuf would not forget the abject look in her eyes and her stifled sobbing.

When spring came and the sky was again cloudless, and the sun shone warmly, and the trees were clothed in green leaves, his feet would lead him to the vegetable market, where he would walk about slowly, listening to the calls of the vendors. Suddenly he would catch sight of a girl carrying a cloth bag, engrossed in haggling with one of the vendors. Yusuf would draw back in agitation: "It's my sister," he would tell himself. He would finger the handle of the knife as he watched his sister; she was a young and tired woman, miserable yet happy at one and the same time. Yusuf would remember the day when he was ill; he was lying on his back and groaning in pain, and when he opened his eyes he saw his sister close by him, crying silently.

She would walk off carrying her bag filled with vegetables, and a porter would come up to her and offer to carry the bag and she would refuse. Yusuf would say to himself, "The young housewife wants to save money."

He would follow her, and when she came to an empty street he would approach her till his shoulder was touching hers, and she would turn round to see who it was and would be surprised to find her brother. Rooted to the spot, the bag of vegetables would slip from her fingers. Looking at him with eyes filled with sadness, humility, and tenderness, she would stretch out her hand to him, and Yusuf would feel that she wasn't his sister but rather some woman friend who had journeyed a long way, and here she was now returning and holding out her hand to him in greeting. Yusuf would stretch out his own hand with a bemused gesture, then they would continue standing together without saying a word. A young man would pass by and would glance at them slyly as though saying to himself, "They are a couple of young lovers," and Yusuf would bend down to take up the bag of vegetables and would ask her gruffly, "How are you living?"

"I married a young man who's poor."

Yusuf would be at a loss for words, though he would understand what had happened: a young man, poor and good-hearted, and a girl who wanted to have a life—and a father who wouldn't give his daughter in marriage to a pauper.

They would walk together till his sister would come to a stop at the entrance to a building and would say, "We're there," and Yusuf would know she was living in the basement. He'd put the bag of vegetables on the ground while his sister was opening the door, then once again he'd take up the bag and make his way inside and immediately he'd be met by the smell of two beings sleeping in one bed and who laughed and quarreled and yet didn't go to sleep feeling sad for themselves.

Yusuf would throw himself into a chair. How comfortable it would be! Once again he would finger the knife. He would get up and unsheathe the sharp-bladed knife and, grasping his sister's hair and throwing her to the floor, would cut her throat as she mouthed in hardly audible terror, "Brother, brother!"

Yusuf would remember the days when he and his sister were small, he being a few years older. Once she had come to him in tears and told him that the neighbor's boy had hit her and he had at once hurried off into the lane and beaten him.

Yusuf would say to the knife, "Die. Stay far away from blood," and his sister would come and stand in front of him, having taken off her coat. What a lovely dress she would be wearing! The dress of a woman who had her own house. She would say to him, "How's Mother?" Yusuf would remain watching her in silence and suddenly she'd burst out sobbing and mutter, "It's all Father's fault. I'll never forgive him. He tortured us so much; he tortured and tortured us."

Yusuf would release his grip on the knife, take his hand from his pocket, and place it under her chin; he would raise her face to him and it would be wet with tears. He would dry them with his handkerchief, saying, "Don't cry," with gentle tenderness, and perhaps she'd jump up and kiss him on the cheek, and there would course through his veins a tempestuous song of joy. Maybe he'd say to her, "Come on, give us a smile."

On returning home he would find the snake lying dead and cold in the courtyard, and he would look triumphantly at his mournful father.

Yusuf was overwhelmed by a strangely violent feeling of sympathy as he lay stretched out on the bed; he would have liked to get to his feet and turn on the light and stare into the mirror.

The music-lovers came, but without their drums and trumpets. Their voices as they chanted were like an endless green plain.

Yusuf gave himself up to a deep sleep, while from the courtyard came the melancholy mewing of a cat, like a call of entreaty for someone to return. Outside the room the snow was still falling, cloaking the buildings, streets, and people in a white mask.

The Family

On reaching his house Abdullah gave a sigh of relief. He looked through his pockets for the key but didn't find it. He rapped with his fist on the old wooden door, with his back becoming ever more bent. He waited, with trembling hands and feet, till the door was opened by a woman in the prime of life, fair-skinned and beautiful, with black hair and green eyes. Abdullah stared at her in amazement. "What are you standing there for?" she said to him. "Why don't you come in?"

Convinced he had made a mistake, Abdullah knocked at the door of another house and enquired in confusion, "Where's Aisha?"

The woman laughed. "What's wrong with you?" she said. "Don't you know me? I'm Aisha . . . Aisha your wife."

"Are you Aisha?" said Abdullah in astonishment.

"Of course I'm Aisha," said the woman. "If I'm not Aisha, then who am I?"

"But Aisha's an old woman," said Abdullah.

"How right was the man who said that people get feeble-minded when they grow old," said the woman. "Listen, man— have you lost your mind? Look at me. Am I a young girl? Look. This hair of mine doesn't have a single black hair in it. Come in, come in and stop your chatter."

Abdullah entered the house with unhurried, troubled steps, eager for his bed. However, he came to an abrupt halt in the courtyard as he heard a shrill scream emanate from one of the rooms. He opened the door and a young girl, breathless and with disheveled hair, ran out; she was being chased by a young man brandishing an ax and shouting, "Give me my ball."

"What's all this?" shouted Abdullah. "Shame on you! Squabbling about a ball as though you were two young children!"

Paying no heed to what he said, the young man hurled himself at the girl and brought the ax down on her head, cleaving it in two.

"What have you done?" screamed Abdullah, distraught. "You've killed your sister."

"She stole my ball," said the young man.

Abdullah seated himself on the ground by the young girl, sobbing and repeating, "Oh my little daughter . . . my little daughter."

Suddenly the little girl gave a long scornful laugh. "Then you haven't died," Abdullah said to her. "Why are you laughing?"

"Look into the mirror," said the girl. "You're crying and your tears are mixing with your snot."

Abdullah looked upward and found that the sky was a gray-colored cloud that was lit up. He closed his eyes and leaned his back against the wall; he heard voices whispering, "He's died and has brought peace to himself and to others."

He heard his son say, "He's left us nothing but debts."

He heard his daughter say, "What shall we do now?"

He heard his wife say, "We must hurry up and bury him."

He heard his son say, "I'll dig a grave."

After a while he heard the powerful, persistent blows of a pickax striking the ground of the courtyard. He sobbed soundlessly.

When he was taken up and placed in a shroud he did not attempt to call for help but gave himself up to the earth which, dark and heavy, was piled upon him.

The Stale Loaf

Abbas wandered round the streets for a long time; the doors of the shops selling bread were all closed, for wheat had long ago become unavailable, the earth not having answered man's cry for help.

All of a sudden Abbas was astonished to see a young boy emerging from one of the houses carrying in his hand a white loaf. Abbas came to a stop, frozen for an instant where he was as he watched the boy, then he pounced upon him. Snatching the loaf from his hand, he fled away followed by a scream of distress.

Abbas returned home and securely locked the door of his room behind him. Then he seated himself on the edge of the bed, breathing heavily, his eyes fastened on the loaf of bread.

His fingers touched the loaf tenderly and he breathed in its aroma. He would moisten it with a little water, then wait for it to soften and regain its freshness, at which he would swallow it down, munching one little piece after another.

Suddenly there was a knocking at the door. He cowered,

holding his breath, his hands grasping the loaf, while the knocking continued.

"Abbas . . . Abbas . . . ," a voice called.

Abbas knew at once whose voice it was, but even so he asked with feigned ignorance, "Who is it?"

"It's Leila."

Leila, his cousin, was a beautiful girl with a pallid complexion, loving silence and living in their house since the death of her parents some months back. How Abbas had suffered through Leila being in love with his elder brother, who had traveled to a distant city in search of work!

Abbas heard Leila's voice calling out, "Open the door!"

"Go away—my mother might see you."

The mother was ever engaged in watching Abbas and preventing him from approaching Leila, while Abbas was always wanting to be transformed into air that Leila might breathe him in so that he could be lodged right inside every cell of her body. Leila was scared of him and a defiant aversion to him looked out from her eyes, as though Abbas was a bull about to attack and rip her open with its horns.

"Open the door."

Abbas approached the door and pressed his face against the wood. He didn't attempt to open it and his hands kept hold of the loaf.

Leila rapped anew at the door and called out insistently, "Abbas . . . Abbas . . . . Open the door."

"Go away. My mother might see you."

"Open the door."

"What do you want?"

"Your mother's not at home."

Abbas gave a sigh of relief, while Leila went on saying in a trembling voice, "Open the door."

"What do you want?"

"I want to see you."

"And what do you want of me?"

"I want to come in."

"I'm not opening the door."

"I'm hungry."

"My room's not a provision store."

"I saw the loaf."

"The loaf is mine." Abbas's voice was gruff.

"I'm hungry."

"The loaf is mine. It's my own."

"Give me a little piece to eat."

"You can die of hunger!"

Leila was silent for some moments, then in an agitated voice said, "Don't you love me?"

"I shan't give you a single mouthful."

"Don't you love me?"

"No, I don't."

Once again there was silence, then Leila enquired dejectedly, "Don't you love me a little?"

"What would you give me if I gave you the loaf?"

"You'll give me the loaf?"

"I'll give you the whole loaf."

"I'll give you anything you ask."

"I'll do with you what I want," exclaimed Abbas.

"Open the door."

"You know what I want of you?"

"Open the door."

"I shall kiss you."

Leila stayed silent.

"I'll rip off your clothes."

Leila stayed silent.

"I'll devour your flesh."

Leila stayed silent.

"You won't tell my mother or my brother."

"Open up—I'm hungry."

Abbas opened the door and Leila quickly slipped inside; at once she fixed her gaze on the loaf held in Abbas's hand. Hurriedly hiding it behind his back, he went toward Leila, who retreated, saying, "First, give me the loaf."

"I'll not give you the loaf. You might scream or run away."

"I'll not run away."

"I'll give you the loaf afterward."

Leila gazed at him beseechingly. "Give me the loaf," she said.

Abbas's fingers tightened their grip on the loaf. He felt a strange strength sweeping through him. "I'll put it on the table," he said, "and you'll take it when it's over."

Abbas moved toward the table, put the loaf on its surface, then went back toward Leila. He stood facing her, his feet apart, staring at her voraciously. So this was Leila. How he had suffered because of her! He had dreamed that one night he would butcher his mother and his brother and bury them in the courtyard, then go back and embrace the sleeping Leila with hands dyed red with blood.

Abbas rushed toward Leila and put his arms round her waist. She resisted so hard that he was forced to let her go. He glowered and said angrily, "I won't give you the loaf."

Leila continued to stand, hesitant and confused, then she approached Abbas and clung to him, and once again he squeezed her in his arms and began kissing her face, hair, and neck. He forced her down onto the rug where they lay stretched out, their faces touching. He closed his mouth over her lips. At once Leila was assailed by a taste that gave her a feeling of nausea—the pungent taste of tobacco. She tried to struggle but his mouth remained clinging to her lower lip. Then, little by little, she began to find the new taste pleasant and wished that it might be intensified.

A feeling of peace growing deep inside of her delighted her, for the loaf would be hers, though she would share it with Abbas.

Sharp, relentless sensations took hold of her, drowning her in a state of fresh alarm. In a breathless voice she muttered, "Leave me. I'll scream."

"Scream"—and Abbas savored the taste of the soft, moist lip.

At that instant there surged through Leila's veins a song, a song without words and with a savage beat. When his mouth seized her breast, cold ice ran through her flesh, then an aged summer's sun shone out. She was immersed in an overwhelming tenderness; she felt that Abbas was merely her child and wished that the milk might flow in her breasts and gush into his mouth.

She heard Abbas say to her, "Open your eyes."

Obeying, she looked at him. Her eyes were overflowing with sweetness—the look in them was like a wingless dove—and Abbas's craving to see her body naked became magnified like a fire that devours forest trees. He began stripping off her clothes and she offered no resistance; she submitted as does a child to its mother's hands. Her underclothes were dirty, old, and torn.

Her white flesh glowed in its nakedness; the body's daytime sparkled. Abbas's hands stretched out and clumsily removed the green ribbon that bound her hair, and the hair dropped down in chaotic profusion, its night mingling with the daytime of the youthful body.

In a trembling voice Abbas said, "Hug me."

She encircled his neck with an arm while the fingers of her other hand pressed into the flesh of his hip.

"Tell me you love me," said Abbas.

"I love you."

"Say 'my darling' to me."

"My darling."

"Kiss me."

Leila began giving him quick short kisses one after the other and Abbas tumbled down into a world ablaze, a world possessed by Leila. He tried to gain control and beseechingly called upon his craving for Leila, his former hunger for her body, and yet he remained incapable of being a man and perceived that he was nothing but a spiritless, impotent being, trembling in agitation.

Leila, stretched out beside him, clung to him, her eyes tight-closed. It seemed to her that she could hear the thundering of a herd of enraged bulls, and she waited open-mouthed, intoxicated, for their approach. Abbas, confused and embarrassed, looked toward the table where the loaf lay. As he touched the soft flesh, he went on imagining to himself the loaf moistened with water, giving out the odor of fields watered by heavy rains. His confusion increased. He heard Leila whisper, "My darling . . . my darling."

She clung to him tighter and tighter. His embarrassment grew ever greater. Flesh had lost its ability to excite. Unable to wait, Abbas freed himself from Leila with an abrupt movement. He jumped to his feet and, snatching the loaf from the table, moved toward the door.

Leila was able to grasp hold of Abbas's foot; he gave her a hard kick in the stomach and she fell on her back. In utter nakedness, she howled with pain.

Abbas left the room and crossed the courtyard at a run. He opened the front door, then slammed it behind him and hurried into the alley. Having put distance between himself and the house, he stood for a while, resting his back against a mud wall, while his fingers avidly grasped the loaf.

The Water's Crime

One day a long time ago a king gazed at a flood of water flowing across a wide space of land, and he asked his vizier in astonishment, "Why does the water tremble?"

"In fear of our august majesty," said the vizier.

"I am not convinced by your answer, which oozes flattery," said the king.

"I have said only what I believe to be the truth," said the vizier.

"As only the guilty tremble in fear, can you inform me of the crime the water has committed?" said the king.

The vizier relapsed into silence and made no replay, so the king summoned his Chief of Police. Pointing at the water, he asked him, "What's that?"

"Water," said the Chief of Police.

"Do you think I'm blind?" said the king irritably. "I'm asking you concerning the information you have about this water."

"It gushes forth from a mountain and comes to the earth and the people," said the Chief of Police.

The king's anger flared. "What an idiot you are!" he shouted. "Do you think I'm a schoolboy? Or have you forgotten you're my Chief of Police? I am asking you about its attitude toward your king."

The Chief of Police was upset. His face became pale and he muttered some incomprehensible words, at which the king said to him, "You and your men are nothing more than robbers and cheats and you don't deserve the salaries you take at the end of every month."

The face of the Chief of Police became more pallid. Before he was able to speak the king said to him in a voice that was like the blade of a sword about to fall upon someone's neck, "Shut up! Do you dare to speak after I have abundant evidence showing that you have neglected your duties? Is not your duty to protect the country from its enemies and to uncover them?"

The king gave a short scornful laugh and enquired, "Have I, the king, become responsible for uncovering the guilty and the conspirators?"

The king ordered that the water be put under arrest. His order was carried out with much vindictive cruelty, the water being incarcerated in a prison that had no doors or windows.

From that time on the prisoner was named the river.

One day a small bird alighted on the bank of the river. It drank from its water, then said, "I am very sad."

"And I'm sad too," said the river.

"I'm sad," said the bird, "because I was chased out of the nest where I lived by a bird that was stronger than me."

"Your sadness will come to an end if you get back your nest," said the river, "but my sadness will not cease unless my enemy the king, who deprived me of my freedom, perishes."

"The king? The king?" said the bird. "Where have I heard this word before? Ah, I remember—I believe my grandfather once told me a story about a king."

"Come on and tell me this story," said the river, "because I love to listen to stories."

Said the little bird: "In olden times some men and women came across land that had much water, wheat, sheep, birds, and trees. They saw that it was suitable for living in, so they built houses and schools and hospitals and children's parks. There they lived a happy and peaceful life until one day there came to their land a stranger carrying a sword. They stared with astonishment and curiosity at the thing he was carrying, for they had never seen a sword before. The stranger brandished his sword, saying, 'This is called a sword. With a single stroke it can cut through any of your necks, so if you are keen to preserve your lives you must submit to my will.' Once again the stranger brandished his sword threateningly and the ears of wheat and the trees and the birds, the women and children and sheep and men all trembled, and by bowing their heads they proclaimed that they were his slaves who would obey his every order.

"The stranger who was the owner of the sword lived in their land, having turned the men and the children and the birds into servants, and the women into slave girls.

"One young man who was known for his courage, having lost patience with having to endure such ignominy, made his way stealthily one night to the king's chamber as he lay in a deep sleep. Stealing his sword, he ran to the river with it. But just as he was about to throw the sword into the water he suddenly became rooted to the spot, thought for a while, then smiled joyfully, for now the days of ignominy had passed and the time for vengeance had come.

"When the next day's sun rose the earth came to know a new king, one who not only brandished his sword threateningly but who also stained it with the blood of men, women, and trees.

"Since that day the stealers of swords increased. Then some of them were forced to take up the making of swords as an occupation, and the number of swords and kings, and of slaves and slave girls grew greater."

All of a sudden the little bird fell silent as it glimpsed a kite hovering in space. Then it took to flight and the river asked itself in bewilderment, "Is there more to the story or is that the end?"

The river liked the little bird's story and went on repeating it unceasingly in a loud voice. As for the people, who were ignorant about the river's language, they called its sound "the babble of water."

A Lone Woman

Aziza was a beautiful young woman. She was frightened of black cats and from the moment she seated herself opposite Sheikh Sa'id she was disturbed. His eyes were two pieces of savage blackness that encompassed Aziza, who was trying to escape from a terror that was very gradually increasing, while the smell of the incense that rose from a brass container filled her nostrils and slowly numbed her flesh.

"So you want your husband to return to you?" said Sheikh Sa'id.

"I want him to return to me," said Aziza hesitantly.

Sheikh Sa'id smiled as she continued to speak dejectedly, "His parents want to marry him off to a second wife."

Throwing some small bits of incense into the glowing container, Sheikh Sa'id said, "Your husband will return to you and he will not marry a second wife."

His voice, calm and grave, gave Aziza a feeling of security and she let out a long sigh of delight. The sheikh's face beamed at her. "But my work," he said, "will require much money."

Aziza's face looked despondent. Gazing at a gold bangle on her wrist, she said, "I'll pay you what you want."

The sheikh gave a short sharp laugh, then said, "You will lose a little but you will gain your husband. Do you love him?"

"No, I don't," Aziza muttered bitterly.

"You've fallen out with him?"

"I've quarreled with his parents."

"Do you feel a tightness in your chest?"

"Sometimes I feel as though there were a heavy stone on my chest."

"Do you have unpleasant dreams when you go to sleep?"

"Always at night I wake up in terror."

The sheikh shook his head several times. "Your husband's parents must have put a spell on you," he said.

Aziza called out in alarm, "What's to be done?"

For a while Aziza was speechless, then she put her hand to her bosom and extracted ten liras and gave them to Sheikh Sa'id, saying, "This is all I have."

Sheikh Sa'id got up and let down the black curtains over the two windows that overlooked the small winding lane, then reseated himself in front of the brass container in which embers glowed above fine white ashes, and began throwing in incense and saying, "My brethren the djinn hate the light and like darkness, for their homes are under the ground."

Daytime outside the room was a woman with white flesh, and the sun's yellow light burned hotly in the alleys, mingling with the clamor of people, while Sheikh Sa'id's room was dark and silent.

"My brethren the djinn are kind. You will be lucky if you gain their love. They love beautiful women. Take off your wrap."

Aziza removed her black wrap and her mature body, in its tight dress, was made visible to the eyes of Sheikh Sa'id. He began reading in a low, indistinct voice from a book with yellow pages, then after a while he said, "Come nearer . . . . Stretch yourself out here."

Aziza lay down close to the incense container. Sheikh Sa'id placed his hand on her forehead, while he continued to recite strange, resonant words. All of a sudden he said to Aziza, "Close your eyes. My brethren the djinn will come." Aziza shut her eyes. The sheikh's voice rose loud, harsh, and authoritative, "Forget everything."

The sheikh's hand touched her face. She remembered her father. The sheikh's hand was rough and had a strange smell; it was a large hand and was certainly heavily wrinkled. His voice was strange, rising louder and louder in the silent room with the mud walls.

The sheikh's hand reached Aziza's neck. Aziza remembered her husband's hand; his hand was soft and flabby like that of a woman. He worked as a clerk at the grocer's shop owned by his father. On no occasion had he tried to caress her neck gently but would squeeze the flesh of her thighs with voracious fingers. The sheikh touched her with both hands. His hands were gently stroking her full breasts and descending to the rest of her body, then returning to the breasts. Losing their gentleness, they pressed down on them hungrily. Aziza moaned and with difficulty opened her eyes to see wispy smoke spreading across the room's void.

Sheikh Sa'id removed his hands and went on reciting and throwing incense onto the embers burning in the brass container. "My brethren the djinn will come," he said. "They will come."

A fierce tremor went through Aziza's body; she closed her eyes and heard Sheikh Sa'id say in a voice that came to her from afar as though from another world, "My brethren the djinn love beautiful women. You are beautiful and they will love you. I want them to see you naked when they come, and they will take away from you every spell."

"No, no," Aziza whispered in panic.

Immediately there came to her the sheikh's voice, like a stern echo, "They will harm you if they do not love you."

Aziza remembered a man she had once seen in the street. He was bellowing like a wounded animal and had then thrown himself to the ground, white foam on his mouth, and had begun moving his arms and legs like someone drowning.

"No . . . no . . . no."

"They will come."

The incense grew thicker, the smell more pungent. Aziza began breathing heavily. Suddenly Sheikh Sa'id called out, "Come, come, O blessed ones. Come."

Aziza heard soft gay laughter and unintelligible words. She had the sensation that the room was crammed full of numerous dwarfish creatures. Despite repeated attempts, she was unable to open her eyes. Fervent breathing seared her face and a single mouth closed upon her lower lip, avidly squeezing it.

The carpet was rough under her naked back; the incense was thickening and being transmuted into a man who grasped her in his arms and numbed her with his kisses. A hungry fire broke out in her blood, while the mouth moved from her lips to the rest of her body.

Breathing heavily, motionless, Aziza felt her fear dwindle. Leisurely, she experienced a delirium with a new flavor. Smiling, laughing, she beheld white stars and a dark blue sky, yellow plains and a sun of red fire. Aziza heard the purling of a distant river. The river. Far away it was. It would not remain far away. She laughed joyfully. Sadness was a child who ran away from her. Now she was a grown-up child. The neighbors' son kissed and hugged her. No, no—that was improper. When he was employed by the baker, he would hand her loaves of bread as she stood at the door of the house; he had stretched out his hand and pinched the nipple of her small breast. It had hurt her; she had got angry; she had become confused. Where was his hand? Here was his hand once again possessing her body. On her wedding night she had let out a scream, and now she did not scream. She beheld her mother holding a handkerchief wet with blood, which the neighbors viewed with curiosity, and her mother called out, her face showing rapturous joy, "My daughter's among the most honorable of girls . . . . May all enemies die of frustrated rage."

Aziza returned to the yellow fields, fields without water. Clouds on high, the sun was a fire that drew near to Aziza. Aziza languidly writhed, elated, burnt by a cruel heat. The sun was a fire that approached and crept into the blood, and Aziza did not attempt to flee, though her feeling of elation continued to increase until she attained the culmination; then the rains pelted down and her whole body trembled.

After a while Sheikh Sa'id moved away from Aziza's naked body; going toward the windows, he put up the curtains and at once the daytime sun flooded into the room and Aziza's white flesh sparkled in the brilliant light.

Aziza became restless; cautiously, unhurriedly, she opened her eyes and was surprised by the sunlight. She rose to her feet in alarm. "Don't be afraid," said Sheikh Sa'id to her. "My brethren the djinn have departed."

Aziza twisted her body in fatigue; she was tired and uneasy. She collected the first article of her clothing, wishing that she could remain for a long time stretched out without moving, her eyes closed.

Sheikh Sa'id wiped his mouth with the back of his hand and said to her again, "Don't be afraid. . . . They've departed."

Tears welled up in her eyes and at that moment the cry of an itinerant vendor could be heard in the lane; the sound came to her from far away as though it were the weeping of a man in despair who will not die.

Minutes later Aziza was walking alone in the long, narrow, winding lane. When she raised her head, looking up eagerly, she found no bird making its way across the blue and empty sky.

The Enemy

The boys in the Saadi quarter were proud of the fig tree standing at the end of the quarter where lay the unattended patch of ground. They agreed that its fruit should not be picked till it had ripened, and so they tirelessly watched over it. Thus, when they learned that their adversaries, the children living in the Murjan quarter, were coming to make off with the fruit of the fig tree, they were overcome with anger. They began making preparations to oppose them and collected up stones and placed them alongside the walls at a number of places, covering them over with old newspapers, and filled paper bags with fine dust. Then the boys stood waiting in readiness.

Their eyes gleamed when a breathless small boy informed them that their enemies were on the way, but they remained calm and composed.

The boys of the Murjan quarter appeared, walking unhurriedly and unawed; they were carrying sticks, some long and thin, others short and thick.

One of the boys of the Saadi quarter hastened to face up to the boys of the Murjan quarter, saying to them in a loud, impetuous voice, "The fig tree is ours. Go on, get out of our quarter."

The boys of the Murjan quarter answered with curses, and a blow with a stick was aimed at the boy, who quickly dodged it, leaping backwards. Then the battle began, and they pelted the boys of the Murjan quarter with stones; taken slightly by surprise, they drew back to take cover, angrily shouting out insults.

The fine dust that had been packed into the paper bags was hurled at them. A thick cloud of dust rose up, and the sticks carried by the boys of the Murjan quarter were ineffective because so many stones were thrown at them that they were forced to retreat. They did not have the courage to approach close to the boys of the Saadi quarter, who became more daring and courageous as they began to advance toward their enemy, inexorably forcing them back till they compelled them to flee from the quarter.

For a while silence reigned. Stones were scattered everywhere and dust covered the ground. The boys of the Saadi quarter were filled with joy when they realized they were victorious and they began leaping about, yelling and exchanging playful punches. Then, after a while, they quietened down and seated themselves under the branches of the fig tree and talked joyfully about their enemies who had taken to flight. With delight and love they gazed at the fig tree, its branches heavy with ripe yellow fruit. Having consulted among themselves, they decided to pick the fruit on the following day. For a time they were silent yet exhilarated, then they quietly conversed.

"Tomorrow we'll eat figs."

"No, we'll sell them."

"We'll pick them, put them in a basket and sell them in the souk."

"With the money from them we'll buy little birds."

"Birds aren't nice in cages."

"We'll buy a sheep."

"A white sheep."

"And we'll run behind it."

Until evening the boys went on guarding the fig tree, only leaving it when they were assailed by their mothers' shouts angrily calling them back to their homes.

When the boys of the Saadi quarter gave themselves up to sleep, some of them saw the fig tree grow so big that its branches touched the face of the blue sky; they also saw a white sheep bleating and saying meekly, "Follow me to the orchards."

The orchards to which the sheep led them were green and had not been set foot in by the boys of the Murjan quarter; in them were no voices of mothers and fathers, and their trees sang with soft, sweet voices whenever the breeze touched their branches, while the sky was like a mother's breast, flowing with tenderness and love.

The boys of the Saadi quarter woke from sleep in the morning and rushed off to the fig tree. They were surprised to find that all its fruit had been picked. For an instant they froze in grief, then they noisily accused the boys of the Murjan quarter of having stolen the fruit of the fig tree during the night. Later, though, they learned that it was the night watchman who had picked the fruit of the fig tree. Though they exchanged vengeful glances, they remained silent, not daring to utter a word, for the night watchman was a solidly built man with a stern face and thick mustache; from his waist there hung a large revolver and it was in his power to imprison anyone he wanted.

Night arrived, heavy-footed with frowning eyes and forehead. The children returned early to their homes and their mothers did not have to nag them. Gloomily they gave themselves up to sleep, and in their sleep they saw orchards whose earth was without green grass and they heard no bleating from a white sheep.

Hasan as a King

The boys of the Saadi quarter were glad when they saw Abu Mustafa leaving his house, carrying his low wooden chair and making his way toward them. They knew he was coming to sit, as he did every morning, under the branches of the fig tree. Abu Mustafa placed his chair on the ground, then, with a satisfied sigh, sat down, and the boys quickly gathered round him.

Abu Mustafa was an elderly man whose face always wore a smile. The boys began whispering among themselves.

"What is it, children?" Abu Mustafa asked them.

"Tell us a story," the boys cried out.

"What shall I tell you?"

"The story of Shatir Hasan."

Abu Mustafa coughed, wiped his mouth with the back of his hand, then lit a cigarette and drew on it several times and slowly blew out the smoke, while the boys' eyes gazed at him eagerly.

Abu Mustafa started by saying, "Once upon a time . . . ."

He stopped for an instant and asked, "Shall I tell the story or shall I have a sleep?"

The children laughed and shouted in high-pitched voices, "Tell us a story, tell us a story."

Abu Mustafa continued in a quiet voice, "Once in olden times there was a poor man called Hasan. He had no luck, like all poor people, and he failed in all the work he did and was forced to sell his furniture so as to buy food for his wife and seven children. Hasan was unable to bear hunger and poverty and he came to see the world as black, and yet he continued to dream of being a king. He decided to escape, to free himself from misery, and one night he left home while his wife and seven children were asleep. Looking up at the sky, he said, 'You, O God, have created my wife and children, and You will feed them.'

"Hasan left his country and continued walking for many many days, during which he ate of the earth's plants and drank from the waters of rivers. How he rejoiced the day there came into sight the houses of a city! He pushed ahead and drew closer to it, when he found a great crowd of people gathered outside the city. No sooner did they see Hasan than they seized hold of him. 'Let me alone,' shouted Hasan. 'I'm a poor miserable man. What have I done?'

"The people informed him that whenever their king died they would stand on a certain day outside the city, and the first stranger who came from the east they would choose as king; as for the stranger coming from the west, they would cut off his head.

"Hasan became exceedingly frightened and began shouting, 'Have mercy on me. I am a father and I have a wife and seven children who will starve if I die. Let me alone. I want to return home.'

"No one paid any attention to his shouting. Binding his hands behind his back, they forced him to kneel and bow down his head. Then, with a single blow of a sword, they cut off his head, and it flew off and began rolling over and over, while a faint cry came out of the mouth: 'I want to return home.' But Hasan didn't return home and he didn't become a king."

Abu Mustafa stopped talking and for a while gave himself up to silence. He began touching his white mustache, then all at once he said to the boys, "Swear you won't leave your country."

The boys made a pretense of being composed and swore they wouldn't leave their country or dream of being kings, though some of them did so without enthusiasm.

City in Ashes

Along time ago there was a small city that had been built amid spacious green fields watered by the abundant waters of a river, and all its inhabitants went about carrying in their pockets pieces of stiff paper on each of which was written a name.

The inhabitants were a mixture of rich and poor. The rich were pleasant and refined and had white masks and shining shoes; they danced well, spoke suavely, and were adept at bowing gracefully and kissing women's hands; their children would call to their mothers with great tenderness, "Mommy." The poor guffawed coarsely in moments of joy, were constantly spitting, and held the belief that they would be received as guests in God's paradise after their death. They called to their mothers in a voice uncouth and drawn out, "Ma."

Both the rich and the poor paid the greatest respect to the dead. Whenever a funeral passed, people would stop, sadness and fear glinting in their eyes, and some would take part in carrying, for considerable distances, the bier of the nameless dead person.

At the instant of opening their mouths to gobble down the first morsel of food, they would all say reverently "In the name of God the Merciful, the Compassionate," and on finishing the meal would mutter "Thanks be to God, the Lord of mankind."

Whenever a girl sinned in the city, her head would, without hesitation, be severed from her body with a large-bladed knife.

Workers labored for eight hours a day and lovers met furtively in the darkness of cinemas, where their hands clasped passionately. Doctors made a practice of conferring their advice with an air of gravity, "Chew your food well. . . . Go to bed early. . . . Avoid smoking and drinking." The older men used to shake their heads sadly and mumble, "Immorality is rife. . . . Women are wearing trousers. . . . Sons no longer respect their fathers. These are the warning signs that life on earth is coming to an end." On meeting first thing in the morning friends would say to each other, "Good morning."

Despite its small size, this city had a sun that would rise at a specific hour, then, likewise at a specific hour, would set. It also had a night studded with numberless stars, all of which faded in brilliance when the white moon made its appearance.

There was a man who had a name living in the city. His face was a skull with some dry, sallow skin attached to the bones. He had a burning desire to be a flower, a bird, or a travel-loving cloud. Despite the fact that he knew he would never be a flower, a bird, or a travel-loving cloud, he was never overcome by depression. He had, however, grown tired of living by himself in a silent and lonely house. So, during one of his gray moments, he decided to buy himself a woman, a woman who would keep him company and would, with her voice, remove the dust adhering to his days. The man went off to the slave market and chose a woman with large eyes, in whose depths there sobbed a sadness tinged with inscrutable magic. The man paid over the price, saying to himself, "Perhaps she will be able to kill the hedgehog that weeps in my blood."

As they walked along the road the man said not a word to the woman, but on arriving at the house he asked of her, "What's your name?"

"My name's Nada," answered the woman in a low, soft voice that trembled slightly.

The man was sitting near the woman. His rough hands, which were shaking, he had placed on his knees. The blood coursed wildly through his veins. At that moment he wished the woman were lying naked on a sandy shore, her breasts wetted by the warm, salty waters of a blue sea. He asked in an agitated voice, "What country do you come from?"

"I have no country."

He gazed at her intently. "You're beautiful," he said.

Her mouth was some small obscure animal of scarlet color; somehow it seemed to the man that it was the one and only mouth. Clenching his fingers, a harsh spasm ran through him. "Your name's beautiful too," he said slowly.

With an enigmatic smile the woman said, "My real name is Shahrazade."

"Are you Shahrazade?" cried the man, overcome with astonishment.

"I am Shahrazade," said the woman. "Death did not reap me—it was Shahriyar who died."

"Shahriyar did not die," said the man. "He is still alive."

"Ah, my master!" said the woman.

"My kingdom collapsed, O Shahrazade."

"We became parted from one another."

"We lost our way through this great earth."

"I looked for you everywhere."

"Hunger made me weep."

"I was imprisoned in a room whose door was bolted."

"I became a beggar."

"I walked the streets enveloped in a black wrap."

"I dug the ground with my nails."

"I lived as a lone woman in cities inhabited solely by men."

"People spat in my face."

"Men who owned gold bought me."

"I'm a wretched man. Why did you forsake me, O my God?"

"Oh, how we suffered!"

"Yes, how we suffered!"

Fiercely embracing, they wept for a long time. In a choked voice the man whispered, "I love you . . . I love you."

She gazed at him, her eyes moist with tears. In their depths there cried out a passion that thrust its talons inexorably into his flesh. Eagerly he clasped the female body to himself, but no sooner had his mouth touched hers than he heard a scream coming from the street, "The enemy have attacked. . . . Kill. . . . Kill. To war!"

The angry, awesome beating of drums became louder. The man found himself unable to ignore it. Sternly he pushed the woman's body away. "Don't leave me," she cried pleadingly. "Don't fight. Stay beside me."

"Be quiet," said the man. "The lances of the city—my mother—call to me."

He took up his sword that hung on the wall and went into the alleyways where men were fighting in the evening gloom. The man plunged into the thick of the battle, aiming his sword at every chest that presented itself. He was overjoyed whenever the long steel blade slipped in, penetrating with savage movement the softness of flesh.

When the battle ended the man came to a standstill, his body wet with sweat and blood. He was overcome by an intense terror on finding himself the sole man remaining alive. As for the others, their corpses were scattered on the asphalt streets in piles of torn flesh. He threw himself down on the bloodied ground and began weeping bitterly, while the fires swallowed up the city's houses and its dead.

The man ceased his weeping when the fires drew near to him. He hurried to escape from the city, to where lay the spacious fields. From there he looked at the city, which had been turned into a vast mass of red fire glowing in the heart of the black night. He dropped down in exhaustion on the grassy ground and gave himself up to a deep sleep, from which he awoke only with the rising of the sun of a new day.

Silence reigned everywhere. The city was a black smoking heap. The man, hearing a faint sound of weeping, looked around him and his glance fell upon a girl in the prime of life lying on the grass. He went up to her and asked, "Why are you crying?"

"The city has been consumed by fire; everyone is dead."

"Then no one remains."

The girl did not reply but continued her weeping. Again he asked her, "Why are you crying?"

Hiding her face in her hands, she answered, "I'm hungry."

The man left her and set off in search of food. He was overjoyed when he came across an apple tree with branches heavy with fruit. He picked several apples and took them to the girl, watching her with tenderness as she greedily ate them.

He was beset by his longing to be a flower, a bird, or a travel-loving cloud.

"Is the girl's name Shahrazade?" he asked himself.

The girl wiped her face with the hem of her dress and fixed the man with a gaze of deep gratitude.

Her expression was meek. The man remembered the days of his departed childhood and said sadly, "Then we are the only people alive."

The girl remained silent. Her lips, though, parted as though she were on the point of sobbing soundlessly. Seeing a red rose, the man plucked it and presented it with embarrassment to the girl, who accepted it with a shy smile that brought joy to the man and set the most beautiful of songs coursing through his veins.

The man helped the girl to her feet and they walked with unhurried steps toward the dead black city.

All of a sudden they heard a bird sing. They stopped and

their eyes met in a long stare. It seemed to the man that he heard the clamor of children tinged with a distant wailing.

The man and the girl continued on their way, their hands clasped in love and affection. Before them was the sun, youthful and radiant.

Nothing

There was the narrow lane with its dilapidated mud walls, there the house, and he gave a sigh of relief as he recovered his breath. He hurried toward the door of the house and pressed the bell. Hearing no ringing, he stood stock-still and at a loss for several moments, then rapped on the wooden door hesitantly. The door was immediately opened to reveal a woman in the prime of life, with large black eyes and disheveled hair, wearing an old nightgown. In a low quavering voice he asked her, "Your husband's at home?"

The woman looked at him hostilely, and said in a husky, jeering voice, "I didn't hear what you said. Who are you asking about?"

"Your husband," he said in confusion.

"Why are you asking about him?" she said.

He said, "I want . . . "

She interrupted him, "What do you want of him?"

"I'm his friend."

"You his friend? I've never seen you before."

"He asked me not to come to him unless it was urgent."

The woman regarded him with keen, searching eyes. "I'm in need of him," he said to her.

"Your friend isn't here," said the woman. "He went away and I've gone to bed."

"When is he returning?" he said, his confusion increasing.

"He left a note to say he wouldn't be away long."

"There's some news he must know about quickly."

"And what's that news he must know about so quickly?"

He didn't reply and the woman said, "Don't you want to speak? The news is secret? I understand—someone's been arrested or is going to be arrested."

She gave a derisive smile which seemed, to his eyes, to be in harmony with her disheveled hair. "Wait for him if you wish," she added, "or go and return after a while."

His eyes roamed over his surroundings, at which the woman said to him in a cheerful voice, "Don't worry. There's no cause for fear. If you would like to wait for him in the house, then enter and look upon the house as your own."

She stepped aside from the door and he entered. When she closed the door he found himself in pitch-black darkness and heard her say irritably, "The bastards have cut off the electricity because we were in arrears."

"I can't see a thing," he said.

"Give me your hand."

He stretched out his hand toward where the voice was coming from. Taking hold of his hand, she laughed and said, "The blind leading the blind." The woman led him into a room whose door she opened with a kick. It was a small room to which the sunlight entered from a single window.

The woman didn't let go of his hand. He became distastefully aware that her hand was sticky and moist with sweat, yet he did not attempt to withdraw his own.

Calling attention to her surroundings with her free hand, the woman said in a grave tone, "This is the palace in which we live. See how huge and grand it is! It's just a single room."

She gave a harsh laugh like that of a drunken man, then continued in an apologetic voice, "I'm sorry. My memory's weak—there's also a lavatory. Would you like to see it?"

He shook his head and she let go of his hand. She stretched herself and yawned, while he stared about him. It was a square room and contained a lone bed, and a table on which were piled many books, magazines, and newspapers; there was also a clothes rack on the wall where women's and men's clothes hung in disorder.

Confused, he remained standing, for he found no chair. The woman pointed with her index finger at the bed, saying, "Sit down. Are you going to remain standing?"

He seated himself on the edge of the bed. She sprawled out on the bed and again yawned loudly. "I'm still in need of sleep," she grumbled.

After some moments it seemed to him he could hear her breathing regularly and he concluded she had gone to sleep. However, she suddenly struck him on the hip with her foot and said, "Are you dumb? Why don't you speak? You haven't told me your name."

He moistened his lips with his tongue and remained silent, staring at the window open to blue space.

"I understand," said the woman. "Your name too is secret."

"My name is Yahya."

"Is that your secret name or your real one?"

Yahya didn't answer. "Tell me honestly," continued the woman inquisitively, "How did you become one of them when you're so young?"

Though he opened his mouth he found nothing to say. The woman said scornfully, "You're miserable and funny. Do you want to change the world? Come along and hurry up before we die like rats."

"The future . . .." " said Yahya in a low voice.

"Shut up!" said the woman angrily. "Don't talk to me of the future. I'm fed up with being lectured to. Do you have a mother and father?"

"My father's dead."

"Are you a student?"

"I work in a textile factory."

The woman lapsed into silence for a while, then said cheerfully, "You've got a beautiful face and it would be easy for women to fall in love with you. Come along and tell me, has anyone fallen in love with you? Don't you have some neighbor's daughter? Speak out and don't be shy. Haven't you known any woman?"

"Only one," said Yahya.

"And how much did you pay her?" said the woman.

He stared at her in confusion, and she said, "Do you think I'm stupid? Look, your face has become the color of blood. I'm certain you weren't on your own and that you had with you three or four of your friends and that you picked up a woman from the street and paid her everything you had in your pockets. Ha, ha, so you became one of them so as to get women free of charge? Ugh! Your silence is irritating. For certain, though, when you attend one of their meetings, you don't persist in keeping your mouth closed but talk on and on till the ceiling sweats. If I'm lying, tell me, 'You're lying.'" He uttered not a word. After a while the woman's breathing became composed. He resumed staring at the window; its bars made him shudder and he pressed his teeth against his lower lip in order to curb a sudden breathlessness that was similar to that of an old man who has been running for hours.

He became aware that the woman's breathing had become agitated. He found himself looking at her; she still had her eyes closed, though her lips were open, while her body was moving as though a man were lying on top of her. Faint intermittent moans came from her. He turned his face away in alarm and started to get to his feet, but he was unable to move. Then he heard the sound of her teeth clenching and unclenching as short rapturous cries emanated from between them. He closed his eyes and beheld the earth's humans crawling along on all fours and being assailed with whips and animal screams. He beheld his grandfather being decapitated, his skin being flayed and stuffed with straw; he beheld his father crying as the muzzle of a revolver was pressed against his temple and fire spurted from it. He quivered and his fingers clasped the hilt of an imaginary knife, and he beheld machines that obliterated old houses and built in their place new ones that were like green trees in a spacious meadow whose ground was covered with roses of bright and varied colors; and he beheld men laughing and women laughing and children laughing; and he beheld the sun that had been transformed into a woman with golden hair walking slowly along a street and gently pushing ahead of hear a pram; and he beheld prisons being pulled down and gallows being burnt and guns and rifles being melted down, and cooking pots and children's dolls being made of them, and he was immersed in a tempestuous exultation that gave him the sudden strength to rise to his feet. He looked pityingly at the woman lying on the bed and left the house, slamming the door behind him and giving a sigh of relief. But several men with scowling faces surrounded him. He knew at once who they were and what they were up to. He said to them in a voice that he tried his best to keep calm, "What do you want?"

One of them, with sleek hair and smart clothes, said, pointing to the door of the house, "We want to thank you for guiding us to this house; we also want from you many other things you will learn of later on."

Yahya gazed at him in bewilderment, and the smartly dressed man laughed and said, "You're surprised? We were of course keeping an eye on you and following you, and you, like a frightened donkey, didn't notice us."

The well-dressed man pointed at two of his men and said sternly, "You and you, take him. If he escapes from you I'll skin you alive."

"Be sure, sir—if he dares to so much as breathe we'll shoot him," said one of the two men.

"I don't want him dead, you idiot," said the well-dressed man irately.

Then he patted Yahya's shoulder as though he were an old friend and said, "As for you, be calm and don't get upset. If you're longing to see your comrade whom we've worn ourselves out looking for, we are awaiting him and you will meet up with what is left of him."

Yahya walked off with bowed head between the two men, and he beheld men sleeping with his sister without her resisting; he didn't shout for help but merely looked up at the blue sky as though he were thirsty and wanted a drink of cold water. One of the men prodded him violently and enquired, "What are you looking at? Are you expecting an airplane belonging to your comrades to come and rescue you?"

"For sure he's bidding farewell to the sun," said the second man.

Yahya smiled and the first man said to him derisively, "Come along and make yourself a hero and smile as they do in films."

Yahya slowed down and indicated a shop that sold cigarettes. "I want to buy a packet of cigarettes," he said.

"It's not allowed," one of the men said.

"Why not also ask to buy yourself a bottle of whisky?" said the other man.

"I'll buy each of us a packet of cigarettes," said Yahya.

"Do you hear?" said the first man to the second man. "He wants to bribe us."

"Do you want my opinion?" said the second man, laughing. "It's best to agree to his request so we can strike a blow at the enemy's budget."

"Go and buy three packets of cigarettes," said the first man to Yahya, "and you might as well know that we smoke only the finest brands."

Yahya bought three packets and gave a packet to each of the two men. However, no sooner had he torn open his packet, extracted a cigarette, put it in his mouth and was about to light it than the first man said to him, "Smoking's not allowed."

"Didn't we agree?" said Yahya.

"We agreed for you to buy cigarettes but we didn't tell you that we agreed to your smoking."

"Just one cigarette," said Yahya.

"It's not allowed."

"Have pity on him," said the second man. "Don't you see he's yellow in the face from fright? Let him smoke a cigarette to pluck up his courage."

"I'm not afraid," said Yahya.

"When, poor fellow, you know what's going to befall you," said the first man, "you'll not just feel fear but will wish your mother had borne a rat rather than you."

"Be nice and tell him what's going to happen to him," said the second man.

"And why shouldn't I tell him?" said the first man. "Is one not a brother to one's fellow man?"

Then he gazed at Yahya searchingly. "Listen, boy—what's your name?"

"Yahya."

"Listen, Yahya. You'll no sooner arrive than you'll be met with punches, slaps, and kicks till your face becomes a hunk of meat at which your beloved would close her eyes in disgust. Then your feet will be placed in the stocks and you'll be bastinadoed till you're forced to bark like a dog, and after that you'll be asked for your name."

Yahya remembered his ancient socks with holes in them and imagined his torturers mockingly laughing at him. He felt real fear and his strength failed him. "What's wrong with you?" one of the men said to him. "Take courage and don't fall down and tire us out with carrying you. The car's close by."

Yahya's fear increased and suddenly he found himself leaping forward and running with all the strength he possessed. He was chased by angry cries ordering him to stop, followed by the whine of bullets. But he continued running, while the mud houses on both sides of the lane grew closer and closer.

Sheep

A number of the men of the Saadi quarter stared aghast on the day they beheld young Aisha, the daughter of Abdullah al-Halabi, walking along, head held high, without an outer back wrap, nothing covering her head but a black and red kerchief. When Aisha had vanished from their sight, they shook their heads sorrowfully and were overcome by a deep feeling of disapproval. Directly night fell they hurried off to the house of Sheikh Muhammad, kissed his veined hand and stared with love and respect at his long white beard. One of them then told him about the action of Aisha the daughter of Abdullah al-Halabi. Sheikh Muhammad was astonished and said, "I don't believe what I hear. Abdullah al-Halabi is a pious and upright man who does not miss a prayer. How right was he who said that the rose gives birth to a thorn."

In a tone of entreaty one of the men said, "What shall we do, O sheikh? Guide us."

"Speak to her father or to her brother," said Sheikh Muhammad.

On the following day the men spoke to her young brother, telling him that his sister had been seen walking in the quarter without an outer wrap. He said to them that his sister had become a student at the university and that it wasn't reasonable she should go to the university wearing a black wrap. They told him that the quarter was indignant at his sister's action, for all the women of the quarter wore wraps. He told them that they should concern themselves with their own wives and daughters, and that as for Aisha she was his sister and not theirs. Furious, they left him, saying that he was a stupid and irresponsible young man, and they decided to talk to the girl's father. However, the old father told them in a tone of rebuke that he had given his daughter the best upbringing and that he had faith in her behavior and morality; he also enquired of them sarcastically, "If a whore wears an outer wrap, does she become good and respectable?"

The men were distressed and met in the evening at the house of Sheikh Muhammad. They informed him of what had occurred and he shook his head in sorrow and said in a trembling voice, "At the end of time women will give up the outer wrap and will walk in the streets bare-headed; they will be wearing men's clothes and one will not be able to tell the difference between men and women."

Sheikh Muhammad looked at the ceiling and said in an imploring voice, "O Lord, save us from that ill-omened day."

In a single voice the men muttered, "Amen."

A man shouted impetuously, "Our quarter is respectable and shall remain respectable."

"Woman is a depraved creature and if she is given a loose rein she will bring ruin and depravity."

"If we are silent today," said one of the men, "a day will come when we shall find our women have become like Aisha."

"I am an old man," said Sheikh Muhammad. "If I live today I shall not live tomorrow, and if I live this week I shall not live the coming week, and if I live this month I shall not live the month that follows it."

"May you have a long life, O sheikh of ours," said a man.

"May God spare you to be a light for us and for our quarter," said a second man.

Sheikh Muhammad continued what he had to say, "There is no escape from death, and every creature is sentenced to passing away. I have today reached extreme old age and every step I take brings me nearer to the grave. The sensible man in such a state casts aside worldly matters and prepares for the journey to the second life, the eternal life that passes not away. But the word of truth must be said. The outer wrap is a protection for woman and for man. Just imagine what would happen if all women were to walk about without it. Their bodies would be seen with all their features, and if a man looked at them the Devil would tempt him and make him desire fornication." The sheikh gave a prolonged cough; when his coughing stopped he said, "My children and my brethren, he who is silent about something objectionable is like him who has committed the objectionable thing, so do that which you consider is proper, and God is He who brings success."

The men discussed what they should do and finally were of the opinion that the family of al-Halabi must be turned out of the quarter.

On the following day, while Aisha was on her way home, three young men blocked her path. One of them asked her, "Where are you going?" Her brow pursed in a frown, she said, "Why do you ask?"

"Is it forbidden to ask?"

"I'm going home," said Aisha.

"The house won't run away," said the young man. "What about coming along with us?"

The second young man said, "Take a look at us. There are three of us and you can imagine how much you'll enjoy yourself with us."

"Have some shame!" said Aisha angrily.

The third young man said, "What are you angry for? We'll pay you the same as others do—we'll pay even more."

The first young man said, "You're a girl from our quarter? Ough! We thought you were a foreigner, for the girls of our quarter don't dress as you are dressed."

The third young man said, "Leave her today, men. We'll see her tomorrow and, whether she likes it or not, she'll come with us."

The three young men moved away from Aisha, laughing. Aisha quickly walked on and entered her home. No sooner had she shut the front door behind her than she burst out crying. Her mother and brother hurried to her and enquired what was wrong. She told them what had happened. The brother promptly left the house and found the three young men still standing nearby, chatting and laughing merrily. Rushing toward them in anger, he said, "Aren't you ashamed? Why did you harass my sister? Don't you have young sisters?"

One of the young men said to him, "Shut up! Someone as vile as you isn't permitted to talk about our respectable sisters."

The brother rushed at the young man and struck him. Retreating a little, the young man drew a knife. The brother was about to fall upon him when the two other young men took hold of him and prevented him from moving; thus his chest became exposed to the knife.

When the sun went down and the darkness of night came, the men of the Saadi quarter lined up in rows behind Sheikh Muhammad and fervently performed the evening prayer. Meanwhile the family of al-Halabi had dressed themselves in mourning.

An Angry Man

Men trembling, packed close together, listening to the reverberation of faraway bombs, their eyes staring anxiously at a stern-faced man who stands in front of them, erect, legs apart, trying not to yield to an overwhelming anger. In a voice that he made an effort to control he said, "I know that my task will be difficult, but it will become easy if you cooperate with me. My task now is to convince you that death is not frightening and is not worth running away from."

None of the men uttered a word. The angry man bit his lower lip and regarded the men with spiteful eyes. Then, in a harsh, cruel voice, he said, "Speak. You must speak." The men remained silent, so the angry man pointed to a man, tall and broad-shouldered, and said peremptorily, "You there—speak!"

"What shall I say?"

"Say what you want to."

"I'm married and if I died who would feed my wife?"

He moistened his lips with his tongue, then added with

embarrassment, "I'm jealous and I love my wife and I don't want to leave her to some other man."

The angry man jeered and pointed to a second man. "And you?" he asked.

"I have five sons and it's my duty to look after them till they grow up and become young men."

"And you?"

"I have nothing in life expect misery, so why should I die?"

"And you?"

"I don't want to die because I have an indescribable love for life."

The angry man shouted, "And because you love life you must die."

Casting a look of censorious rebuke at the men, he continued speaking in a cold voice, "You arc cowards, and if you have not chosen death you will lose what you love."

A strange silence descended. Suddenly one of the men screamed, "You hate us."

An uproar broke out from which emanated impetuous voices.

"We don't want to die."

"We shan't die like dogs."

"Life is better than the grave."

"Die on your own."

"A live coward is better than a dead brave man."

The angry man shouted pleadingly, "I love you. I love all people and because I love you I want you to face the enemy and to die."

"Then go and die if you are not afraid of death."

The angry man plunged his hand into his pocket and took out a dark-colored revolver. The men began recoiling in alarm. "Don't be frightened," shouted the angry man. "I shan't hurt you. You will be killed sleeping in your beds."

He raised the revolver and placed the barrel against his temple. "As I told you, death is trivial and stupid."

He gently pressed the trigger and the sound of a bullet reverberated. The angry man fell to the ground, his head bleeding, while the reverberation of explosions grew gradually nearer and nearer, warningly encompassing them.

The Face of the Moon

The woodman's ax was falling monotonously on the trunk of the lemon tree standing in the courtyard, while Sameeha was sitting by the window that overlooked the alley; from it there rose up from time to time the ravings of a mad young man, mingling with the sound of the ax. The smell of the lemon tree stole into the room, penetrating the air, like a blind beggar-woman knocking at doors in dejected entreaty.

The ravings of the madman grew louder; raucous and disjointed, they reached Sameeha's ears. In them lurked an angry wild animal that called to some creature astir in her veins. It was possible for her to see the madman as he leapt about in the alley, while around him several boys were shouting and pelting him with orange peel. To Sameeha his eyes were like two ailing tigers drowsing on the grass of dark jungles.

Sameeha's father was a man advanced in years and wracked with illness. The scent of the lemon tree troubled him and he had decided to get rid of it, so he had brought the woodman without heeding Sameeha's entreaties, for the lemon tree had been her friend since the days of her childhood. When winter came it became increasingly beautiful with raindrops sparkling on its leaves. Then its greenness appeared lit up, fulgent, as though at any moment it would burst into flame.

The ravings of the madman became louder as though they were the weeping of the lemon tree that would shortly be destroyed. An incoherent fear came to growth in Sameeha's flesh, and it seemed to her that she was in possession of a sky full of pallid lights that were but her dead dreams, for at that moment Sameeha was no more than a woman in the prime of life who had been divorced by her husband some months ago. She could have been a good wife, cooking the food, washing the clothes, cleaning the rooms, and yielding to the man who was her husband, simulating ecstasy, gaiety, and passion. When she was ten years old her father had slapped her hard because he had seen her dress riding up over her thighs, yet when she was to marry, her married female relatives had instructed her in how she should move her body when coming together with the man's, how to become a responsive voice full of answering echoes and sensual yearning for the man. Her husband used to be angry and exasperated with her, for at night, when she was stretched out against him, she would panic and draw back when his hands touched her, would be transformed into flesh that was passive, submissive, and without movement to the weight of a man. The husband had not been able to live with her, for he wanted a woman who would moan and whose flesh would quiver when she breathed in the smell of a man heavy upon her.

Sameeha returned to her parents' house, to lead a life of frustration, helping her mother with the housework, then wiling away the rest of the day's hours sitting by the window and watching the passersby in the alley.

The young madman never left the alley, always screaming and leaping about as he chased after the children.

In those moments the ax's blade was still wounding the trunk of the lemon tree, cutting through its body more and more. The sound of the ax made Sameeha feel that she was losing her childhood little by little. In the old days Sameeha had been a child who laughed without reason. The moon would frighten her and she could not be persuaded that it was merely a disc that gave out a white light.

Sameeha heard a weird shrill scream. Immediately she realized it must be coming from the madman, so she looked out of the window and saw him sitting on the ground, his head held between his hands, while the blood gushed out from between his fingers. The children had taken to their heels after one of them had thrown a stone at him.

Sameeha withdrew from the window, victim of a mysterious terror, and threw herself down on the couch. The perfume of the lemon tree and the sounds of the ax mingled with the screaming of the madman. Sameeha closed her eyes, yielding to severe trembling. She felt that fingers were pressing on her throat and depriving her of air. She wanted to scream for help before she choked. A painful weight crept across her whole body, then withdrew, leaving Sameeha to regain her breath and sense of peace. Sameeha began breathing heavily with a happiness in which was mingled a sort of fear. All of a sudden she caught sight of the mysterious man who used to invade her dreams at night. The man was tall, completely naked, his skin covered thickly with coarse black hair. How strongly she yearned to touch him, but she was unable to move.

The ax was still striking cruelly at the trunk of the lemon tree. The mysterious man smiled; he was standing near the door and his eyes gleamed. In a strangled voice Sameeha said, "Go away."

His lips opened into a wide smile. His teeth looked white, his lips like congealed crimson blood. She wished be would say something. She had a violent desire to hear his voice, which would for certain be like the surging of waves striking against the rocks of a far distant shore.

Sameeha tried to flee as he started to approach her. "Go away," she said again.

The man did not heed her and continued to come closer. He stretched out a hand; the five fingers touched her flowing hair. His lips moved without any sound issuing from them, yet Sameeha was certain that he had said to her, "My darling."

The madman's screaming intensified. Taking Sameeha's hand, the mysterious man drew her along; she followed him without resisting, and a delightful sense of tranquility took hold of her. She knew his hand, knew it well. Where had she seen it before? She didn't remember. She tried to remember. Led by the man, they crossed together rolling plains where meet the snows of winter, the summer's sun and the flowers of spring. They arrived at a dilapidated house. Sameeha knew the house, had seen it before. Where? Where? The darkness was routed and she quickly began to remember—it was a dilapidated, deserted house that used to squat phantom-like at the entrance to the alley in the days when she had been young.

She looked at the man and found that he had changed. Having relinquished his youthfulness, he had become middle-aged. She recognized him at once—she had been not more than twelve years old when she was returning home, and the evening darkness had begun to flow into the lanes. When she had arrived close to the dilapidated, deserted house a middle-aged man had blocked her way and roughly seized her hand. "I'll kill you if you scream," he had said to her in a husky voice.

He had quickly dragged her into the house and stripped her of her clothes. At that time her breasts had not yet ripened, though her flesh was smooth and firm. The man's body had the smell of a dead fire.

Sameeha gazed at the middle-aged man apprehensively, for he had returned to her after protracted waiting. She wanted to rush toward him and lay her head on his chest, but she heard him say to her, "I'll kill you if you scream."

She did not resist; she was bewitched by the extraordinary tenderness flowing deep within her, and she remained lying on her back waiting for the body of a middle-aged man which had the smell of a dead fire.

The madman's screaming rose again. Sameeha, lying on the couch, tried to ignore it, but the screaming continued to grow louder and more raucous and she was unable to bear it. Rising to her feet, she hurried to the window and looked down onto the alley; she found the madman still sitting on the ground; he was struggling with the barber and the grocer, who were attempting to bandage the wound in his head by tying round it a piece of white cloth. Meanwhile his screams turned into the howling of a ferocious animal.

Sameeha did not try to return and lie down on the couch. At this moment it was possible for her to hide herself in the dilapidated deserted house, with the darkness of evening and the middle-aged man.

She gazed at the madman, who was rolling on the ground, moving his arms and legs. She sensed that the middle-aged man had departed and was dying in some faraway place. She wished that the madman might be transformed into a deluge of knives that would inundate her body, slowly rending her flesh, then leaving her face to face with the aged terror.

Sameeha went back to stretching herself out on the couch; she closed her eyes. One day she would be alone in the house and she would entice the madman to enter. Without shame she would strip herself of her clothes and would give her breast to the madman's mouth; she would laugh, intoxicated, as he tried to gnaw at the nipple. In a breathless voice she would ask him to bite her flesh, to sink his teeth into it till the blood gushed forth and stained his lips. Then she would lick his lips with avid tenderness.

For several moments the ax stopped its onslaught, then there rose up the sound of the lemon tree falling and of it striking the ground of the courtyard with a crash that quickly died away.

Sameeha smiled when she remembered the moon, for it would never again terrify her, after she had seen its face unmasked.

Genghis Khan

When Genghis Khan was born, his head had not expected a crown of gold, for his father was poor and respected by no one. His mother was a middle-aged woman; she had sad eyes and had never once laughed from the heart.

Genghis Khan spent his childhood in the alleyways playing with mud and stones. But when he became a young man he was crowned as a king, for hunger had for long tormented him. His love for poetry, so like a child's laughter, had not been vanquished. Always he was smiling, though the desire to weep sometimes gripped him for no reason.

Genghis Khan fell in love with the gentle girl chosen to be the mother of children who had not yet come. On the night when their two bodies came together for the first time, the young girl clung to him, fiercely drawing him to her, and Genghis Khan felt her body as an animal with thousands of mouths, fangs, and talons.

In the morning Genghis Khan left his bed with sullen face,

while the girl was sprawled on the bed, a long-bladed dagger plunged into her chest.

For many days Genghis Khan remained silent and depressed, wandering about his palace like a dark phantom without a head. His ministers and bodyguard watched him, alarmed and perplexed, for they were accustomed to submitting to the will of the person they had chosen as their ruler.

One day Genghis Khan stood among his ministers and bodyguard; he was like a tree that has been uprooted from its soil and has been magically fixed in space. He spoke, giving orders to the leaders of his armies to set forth across the world and to destroy the cities scattered on the face on the earth.

There was one small city with no outer walls whose inhabitants believed that God was to be found everywhere; they were convinced that God had created countless numbers of angels, that they were made of light, had white wings, and could not be seen by human eyes.

Each person was subject to the surveillance of two angels, who recorded his good deeds and his bad, and when the person died the good deeds and the bad deeds were placed in the two scales of a balance and the one that weighed the most determined whether he was to go to heaven or to hell. Hell was a burning fire that tormented without bringing about death, while heaven was a beautiful place filled with green trees, beautiful women, and rivers of honey, milk, and wine.

The inhabitants of the city loved to smoke hubble-bubbles and their heads would sway in rapture the moment a hand struck the skin of a drum.

They would drive cars, for they had not yet discovered horses, which were still untamed, galloping across the deserts.

Genghis Khan's armies found no great difficulty in storming the city. They murdered several thousand of the inhabitants, and Genghis Khan gazed entranced at the corpses of the hanged as though they were twinkling stars.

The houses were searched and the children brought together and slaughtered on the bank of the river, whose waters lost their coloring.

Many months passed, filled with clamor, merry-making, and screaming, then little by little calm began to gain control; the inhabitants regained their love of smoking hubble-bubbles, of playing on drums, and talking about scandals and about God who is present everywhere.

Boredom started to take possession of Genghis Khan, penetrating his flesh like some obscure and frightening disease. One day it caused him to cast off his crown and robes and to steal away in disguise and to roam through the city like a snake in search of flesh. Tired of wandering about, he made his way into a café patronized by a mixture of young men and girls. He ordered a cup of coffee. A song was coming from the jukebox in one of the corners.

Genghis Khan began sipping his coffee and smoking, while the male singer wailed in a hoarse, wounded voice, "I shall die if you leave me."

Genghis Khan puffed smoke from his cigarette as he gazed with curiosity at a beautiful girl near him. She was tapping her foot in time to the hot music. Her hands were lying on the iron table; they were small and excessively white.

Genghis Khan stared at his large coarse hands and a mysterious sadness flowed into his blood, and his nostalgic yearning to hear poems being recited by a hoarse, raucous voice became more intense. He felt his heart to be a wingless bird that longed to fly toward the home in which it had been born, a house with mud walls and an orange tree standing in the courtyard. Genghis Khan gave a sigh of relief; little by little he felt that the flood of children's blood was moving away from him, that the corpses of the hanged were vanishing from his imagination.

Leaving the café, he was certain that Genghis Khan the shedder of blood had died forever and been buried in some distant unknown place, and that his armies would continue to wait for him in vain.

His armies waited for him and searched for him. He had, though, skillfully hidden himself, so, not finding him, they were forced to depart. Elated, Genghis Khan watched the dust rising behind them, then he set forth through the streets as though he were a child just born, for, in the coming days, he would be an unknown man living in a small city. He would find work and read poetry of an evening. He would dream and would fall in love with a girl who'd be like some grown up child. She would love jasmine and the summer, and her body would be sweet laughter. They would live together and she would bear him children, and he would love them because they would be hers. He would haggle enthusiastically with the salesmen when buying things for their home.

Genghis Khan stopped fantasizing when he noticed a large gathering of people jostling around the door of a house. He thrust his way in among them and found a woman screaming and wailing and pointing to a small boy lying by the doorway.

Genghis Khan fixed his eyes on the dead child and saw that his face and limbs had been gnawed by rats. Withdrawing in terror, he slipped from the crowd, controlling a savage desire to weep mixed with a violent rage. He rushed out of the city, for Genghis Khan had come back to life.

There were loud cries of joy from his troops when they saw him approaching. Genghis Khan put on his armor and placed his steel helmet on his head, glancing scornfully at his gold crown. Brandishing his sword, he ordered his armies forward.

As he listened to the clamor of his men, so like an angry storm, it seemed to him he was seeing a flood of molten iron inundating the whole earth, and at this he smiled with satisfaction.

And heaven was still an exceedingly beautiful place filled with green trees, beautiful women and rivers of honey, milk, and wine.

The Day Genghis Khan Became Angry

Genghis Khan was a man of blood and fire. Directly he felt bored he would remember the cities he had destroyed by fire, the men, women, and children, the books, birds, cats, trees, and grass he had wiped out; his boredom would then vanish and in its place there would prevail a feeling of bliss that was like a solitary star twinkling in the nights of the earth's deserts.

But one day Genghis Khan, finding no way of ridding himself of his feeling of boredom, was ravaged by an oppressive sense of helplessness. He was thus forced to seek the advice of one of his viziers famous for his wisdom and sound opinions.

The vizier knitted his brows and said to Genghis Khan gravely, "Give me a few days so that I may think up some effective remedy."

"You speak as though you were a doctor and I a patient," said Genghis Khan irritably. "Answer immediately or I'll order my attendants to skin you alive while you watch what's happening to you."

"There is no cause for anger," said the vizier, "for everything you desire will be realized without delay, and I shall answer . . . . "

Genghis Khan interrupted him, "Come along, give your answer and don't waste time by beating about the bush. I want some method of doing away with the unbearable boredom I feel."

"The reason for your boredom," said the vizier, "may be attributable to your sitting around for long periods in a palace filled with all you desire, and thus a change might possibly free you from boredom."

Genghis Khan thought for a long time, then decided to pursue his vizier's advice. He decided to disguise himself in the kind of clothes worn by poor people and left his palace without any guards or servants. Though he wandered about the streets until his feet were tired and his strength had given out, his boredom, far from leaving him, increased. A black cloud had taken possession of him and he had it in mind to return to his palace to punish his vizier. However, he noticed a man raining down blows with a stick on a donkey and found himself rushing toward the man, seizing the hand that wielded the stick and saying to him furiously, "If your heart were of stone you wouldn't beat your donkey so cruelly."

The man stared at Genghis Khan in astonishment without uttering a word. It was nevertheless the donkey that spoke, addressing Genghis Khan with scornful disapproval, "What's this unseemly meddling? Is it I who am being beaten or you?"

"This is truly extraordinary!" said Genghis Khan. "A donkey that talks!"

"Furthermore," said the donkey proudly, "I talk without the common grammatical errors people make."

Genghis Khan's amazement was increased and he said to the donkey, "And you also speak as cultured people do."

With head high, the donkey said superciliously, "I am cultured, of course."

Genghis Khan laughed and said, "I think it would be best, if you are anxious to speak only the truth, for you to correct your words by saying that you are a cultured donkey."

"You are mistaken," said the donkey, "for, though being a donkey, I am not a donkey."

"What is this strange way of talking?" said Genghis Khan. "Are you giving me riddles to solve or are you asking me to deny what I see and to believe what I hear?"

"You are entitled," said the donkey, "to reject my words and to charge me with such accusations as you wish, but if you knew my story you'd believe what I've told you."

Overcome by curiosity, Genghis Khan said, "And what is your story?"

Said the donkey, "I was previously a human being. I used to read books, papers, and magazines, and would listen to the radio news bulletins, and would watch the television programs. However, I wanted to employ my education in order to attain personal benefits, both material and spiritual, so I was made to walk on all fours. I continued to walk on all fours in the hope of gaining what I aspired to in the way of honor, influence, and wealth, but I did not obtain what I was seeking by reason of the large numbers of those who crawled, and I was transformed into what you see me as now."

"And your ears?" enquired Genghis Khan. "How did they become so large?"

"It's because I used to use them more then my tongue," said the donkey.

Forgetting that he was dressed as a poor man, Genghis Khan said, "When I return to my palace I'll order that your story be written down so that it may be a lesson to those who would take warning."

"You?" said the donkey. "You who look like a beggar own a palace?"

"I not only own a palace," sad Genghis Khan, "but I am

Genghis Khan, lord of the world. Have you not heard of me?"

"I won't believe what you say, not if you were to eat all the books on the face of the earth."

"Why?" said Genghis Khan.

"The answer's simple," said the donkey, "for if you were really Genghis Khan you would not concern yourself with writing down my story but would have ignored it, for the favorite of him who is a ruler is he who is proficient at crawling."

"Your answers are not devoid of an intelligence that qualifies you to be one of my viziers," said Genghis Khan.

"Only now am I convinced that you are Genghis Khan."

"Why?" said Genghis Khan.

"Because it is not surprising," said the donkey, "that Genghis Khan should choose as a vizier someone who was a human being and has been transformed into a donkey."

Genghis Khan became furious and said to the man who was carrying the stick, "I shall order your head to be cut off if you don't carry on beating your donkey cruelly, for it is badly brought up and impertinent."

So the man continued to beat the donkey zestfully, while Genghis Khan made his way to his palace. While his boredom had dispersed, it had been replaced by a seething anger. He commanded the sun to set and its light to pale and, immediately and without hesitation, it obeyed. He also commanded all the donkey-owners to be in possession of sticks and whips and to employ them constantly, and from that day on donkeys have suffered an oppression that will never end.

Room with Two Beds

A hmed and Isam were friends. Both were in the prime of life and lived in a single room in a house owned by a woman whose husband was dead. Though her face was not as beautiful as the moon, yet her body was full of femininity. The room contained two beds, a wooden table, and one chair; there were pictures of women torn out of magazines stuck to the walls haphazardly.

Ahmed and Isam believed that the earth was not spherical, and they had been arguing from early morning till noon and had been unable to come across any convincing proof.

The sun was shining violently outside their room at the moment when Ahmed approached the window and drew the curtain a little to one side with a cautious, furtive movement. "The landlady's started her washing," he said.

Isam hurried toward the window and began peeping out at the landlady, who was sitting in the courtyard on a low stool; in front of her was a large metal basin; steam rose up from the pile of clothes draped in a white soapy foam.

The landlady was humming a song as she rubbed and squeezed the clothes, then placed them in another basin alongside her. Suddenly her dress rode up over her thighs as she moved. Ahmed gave a faint gasp and said, "What merchandise!"

"Don't talk like some old-fashioned trader."

"Everything in the world is merchandise with its price."

"Then you're cheap merchandise."

"And you're a coward. The truth is a steel knife; when it penetrates to your heart you'll comprehend through suffering the true face of the earth."

"Woman will still be a beautiful creature."

"Be a man and leave your mother's breast."

"Look at our neighbor—she's like a cat."

"Cats are very wicked."

"Dogs are better than cats."

"Then go and fall in love with a dog."

"Look. Look. The sun's come out."

At that instant the dress had risen still higher over the thighs of the landlady so that they were revealed naked and exceedingly white; sprinkled with drops of water, they glowed alluringly under the sun. The landlady wiped her hand on her dry dress and brushed aside a lock of black hair from her eyes, then again plunged her hands into the water. She did not attempt to cover her thighs with the dress.

"Look, look at her face—she's smiling."

"She knows we're watching her."

"We'll force our way into her room at night."

"We'll find her asleep."

"We'll bind her mouth with a piece of cloth."

"We'll be deprived of kissing her mouth."

"We'll sacrifice a part in order to gain other important parts—that's life."

"We'll secure her with a rope."

"She'll be as if dead."

"But her flesh will still be warm."

"Who'll be the first?"

"I."

"No, I'll be the first."

"The two of us will attack."

"It'll be a battle."

"An historical battle."

"Historical? Why?"

"We'll tear her clothes to pieces."

"And if she undresses without a struggle?"

"We won't agree. She's the spoils of war."

"Rubbish!"

"She might make a complaint against us."

"Rubbish!"

"We might be humiliated in court."

"We'll say to the judge boldly, 'Does a woman live without a man?'"

"And we'll say to him, 'We want to give happiness to others.'"

"And he'll award us with grand titles and medals."

"Down with titles and medals!"

"We might be put in prison."

"In prison we'd enjoy peace. There we would feel we were living on solid earth. We'd have just one desire: to get out of prison."

"Who knows, she might enjoy what we do to her and then she'd be troubling us every night!"

"Welcome to such trouble!"

"She'd become a beggar."

"We're all beggars."

"I'm hungry and I wish I was a beggar to ask our neighbor to give me a little of that quince jam to eat she made some days ago. Do you remember its golden brown color?"

"Shut up. Look."

At that moment the landlady rose to her feet and took up the basin in which the washed clothes had been piled.

"I wish she had a lot of clothes!"

"Do you want her to go on washing clothes till she dies?"

The two friends moved away from the window and began to get dressed. When they finished Ahmed gave the door of the room several bangs to announce that two men were about to go out and that the women should hide themselves.

The two friends left the house and walked silently through the streets. Then they stopped walking and looked at a woman with a beautiful face and body who was standing near a tree in a state of embarrassment. A few moments later a car came along and stopped beside the pavement. It was driven by a handsome, smartly dressed young man; he opened the car door for the woman who, freed from her embarrassment and with her face lit with joy, got into the car; the engine gave a roar and the car sped away.

The two friends exchanged glances without saying anything. Their faces were dejected.

"Where are we going?" asked Ahmed.

There streamed into Isam's imagination the streets, the cafés, and the cinemas, and the world seemed to him like a cage with steel bars. He couldn't find a word to say. The two friends walked on in silence. Suddenly Ahmed laughed and enquired, "Is the world spherical?"

"It's not spherical."

"But it is."

"No, it's not spherical."

Again they relapsed into silence as they went down into streets full of noise. They turned off into a small restaurant, ate dully, then went to a café they often frequented, where they sipped tea and played cards enthusiastically. Isam lost. Then, while the sun was about to set, they returned to the room and lay down side by side on the bed. The other bed remained empty.

No Raincloud for the Trees,
No Wings above the Mountain

They put him into custody one night just at the moment when he was ripping up a picture stuck to the wall; the picture of a bearded man with a meek face and stern eyes.

They hurried him off to an ancient cellar with dank walls full of tables and chairs. There they gathered round him—frowning faces and eyes that gazed at him with scornful curiosity.

"What's your name?" one of the four asked him.

"Suhail . . . Suhail Badour."

"And your age?"

"I'm twenty."

The man said to his comrades in astonishment. "Look at him. Look, he's more beautiful than a girl."

Another man stretched out his hand, touched Suhail's face and said, "Ah, how soft his skin is!"

"His flesh is all flabby," said a third man.

In a joking tone the fourth man said, "Let's get to work first, men. Have you forgotten we've got to question him, not make a drawing of him."

Smiling, the first man said, "The world won't go to ruin if we put off questioning him till the morning, for, as the proverb says: a time for your heart's desire and a time for your God."

The heads of the four men drew close and they whispered together, laughing with noisy merriment. They informed Suhail of what they intended doing. Taken unawares, he drew back in alarm. At once they threatened him with resorting to force if he refused, and they stood there in front of him, erect and cruel, their eyes wild and brutal, and the air went from his lungs, his voice was lost to him, his strength failed him, and he was transformed into a quivering body with two beseeching eyes.

He was overcome by an all-enveloping feeling of shame, so he closed his eyes and bit his lower lip. He uttered not a word when one of the men asked him in a convulsive voice, "Why did you tear up the picture?"

The man of the picture had said to cities whose backs were bowed, "The life of this world is short-lived and there is naught of good in it. It gives only hunger and troubles. Patience, then, patience, O you who are poor, for yours alone is paradise after death . . . ."

Suhail had seen the earth as a vast green garden with children running joyfully beneath a blue sky, and he had seen the hungry destroying the tombs and building over them houses for themselves in search of sun and the air, and his blood rose up in rage and with impetuous fingers he had torn up the picture of the bearded man with the meek face and stern eyes that had been stuck to the wall. At once he had been surrounded by four men whose car bore him far away from the trees of the streets and the night with its ever trembling stars.

The four men seated themselves on the chairs, smoking cigarettes, while Suhail remained standing without moving, his head lowered, staring at the dirty floor, till they asked him to sit on a chair. He complied, and one of them offered him a cigarette, which he lit with a match, smiling amicably.

The four men talked in discontented voices about the rising costs of bread and meat. To Suhail's eyes they appeared meek and tired, curbing a strong desire to go to sleep. Then, suddenly, one of them rose to his feet and left the room, returning with a blanket which he spread on the floor. He asked Suhail to lie down on it and turned to his comrades, inquiring proudly, "Isn't this a great idea of mine?" Exclamations of approbation came from them.

Suhail threw himself down on the blanket, burying his head in the coarse wool. He shivered as he looked at the earth covered with gallows from which dangled small naked corpses, and waited in expectancy and fear for what was to happen.

Death of the Black Hair

The noonday sun sparkled white on the Saadi quarter while the sheikh of the mosque was telling the worshipers that it was God who had created men and women, and children and birds and cats and fishes and clouds, and it was He too who had created His poverty-stricken servants from earth. The men nodded their heads in agreement, their faces resembling earth upon which not a drop of rain had fallen, and the day they died they would be buried in earth. When the noon prayer ended, the men left the mosque, seized by a quiet humility and gentle melancholy. Most of them made their way to the café in the Saadi quarter where they discussed what had happened a few days ago when Mundhir al-Salim had gone to the police station and, with head held high, had announced that he had killed his sister, for, in the Saadi quarter, dishonor could only be blotted out with blood.

Thus had died Fatma, the fruit of which all trees dreamt, for Fatma was a beautiful woman, but the most beautiful thing about her was her black hair, dark water in which no star twinkled, the tent that gave shelter to the frightened man on the run.

When Fatma was young in years her grandfather used to love to comb out her hair and would let loose her jet-black locks with elation and pride, mumbling in wonder, "What a treasure!"

The day that Fatma entered the reception room with uncertain tread, bearing the coffee cups, the eyes of the matchmaking women were struck by her hair. Their admiration was won immediately, and several weeks later trilling cries of joy rang out and Fatma became the wife of Mustafa, the man possessed of a face that did not smile.

Mustafa loved Fatma and her hair, and he would see in his sleep a single dream in which he would run under heavy rain without being made wet by a single drop.

Mustafa used to say to Fatma, "I'm a man and you're a woman, and the woman must obey the man. Woman has been created to be a servant to man." And Fatma would say to him, "I obey you and do all that you want." And he would slap her and say imperiously, "When I speak you must shut up." Fatma would cry, but like some small bird, gay and frivolous, she would stop crying after a while and would laugh and wipe away her tears, at which Mustafa would close his eyes and imagine Fatma saying to him submissively, "I love you and would die if you left me."

But Fatma never once said what he yearned to hear.

One day Mustafa entered, with scowling face, the café of the Saadi quarter and said to her brother Mundhir al-Salim, "Before you seat yourself like Antar among the men, go and take your sister from my house."

Mundhir al-Salim bowed his head in shame before the men surrounding him, savagely bit on his lip, then abruptly rose to his feet and began running through the Saadi quarter.

When Fatma saw her brother hurling himself upon her, his knife drawn, she gave a scream and fled from the house. She ran in the alleyways of the Saadi quarter, bare-headed, her hair disheveled, calling out for help. But the knife caught up with her and reached her throat, while the men and women and children stood frozen, their faces pale.

Thus died the black hair, yet Fatma still runs in the quarter of Saadi, knocking at the doors of the houses calling for help, but no door is opened to her and the knife is stained with blood.

The Smile

Woken from sleep at dawn, he was taken out of his cell and led to an open space where wooden stakes had been set up at intervals. He was tied to one of them and said in a hoarse voice, "I am not a coward. I do not want my eyes to be bandaged. I want to see what happens."

No heed was paid to his words and his eyes were bandaged with a piece of black cloth, then he heard boots sharply striking the ground. He shuddered and ran to the house in which he was born. He entered, in terror and out of breath. "Mommy . . . Mommy," he called.

No one answered him, and he said to himself, "Perhaps she's asleep."

He made his way to the room in which his mother slept. He found the door open and caught sight of his mother lying naked under a strange man. He sobbed, trembling, and tried to draw back, to disappear, but, unable to, he was frozen to the spot.

Suddenly his mother noticed him. "Have some shame and stop staring like an idiot," she told him in a high-pitched, tremulous voice. "Do you think you're watching a film? Go off and play in the lane and don't come back home till I call you."

Leaving the house, he ran in the direction of the open space where the wooden stakes had been set up at intervals. He was tied to one of them and he said in a plaintive voice, "I don't want to have my eyes bandaged. I want to see how I'm going to commit suicide."

No heed was paid to him and his eyes were bandaged with a piece of black cloth, then he heard a stern voice giving an order, which was followed by the whine of bullets that thudded into his body filling it with gory holes. He gave a sneering smile, but all too quickly a bullet pierced his head and wiped out the smile.

Death of the Jasmine

Salma was able to be appointed as a school mistress after being granted a certificate confirming she had slept with 927 men in one year. She was required to teach the first form, in which there were thirty children, none of whom was more than seven years old.

When Salma carefully opened the door with delight and made her way noiselessly into the classroom, the pupils were shouting and yelling, some of them striking the wooden desks with their fists. However, they all stopped making a noise once they were aware of her presence and began scrutinizing her carefully. Salma was a beautiful young girl, with well-developed breasts and full lips that were always slightly open as though at any moment they were about to whisper some exciting secret.

Silence reigned in the long classroom. Salma placed herself in front of the blackboard and began examining the faces of the children who had from that moment become her pupils. Rapturous joy flowed through her, for her dream to live with children who had as yet not known bitterness and defeat had been realized. A pupil whispered to his companion seated beside him, "Look at her bosom."

"I only look at her two breasts."

"Why?"

"I'm spiritual."

At the back of the classroom there were two pupils talking in low voices, "Where did you go yesterday evening?"

"To a night club—the whisky was atrocious."

He spat in disgust on the floor, then said, "Everything's become atrocious these days."

In a gentle voice Salma said, "This is the first lesson and I shall be teaching you . . . ."

"What will you be teaching us?" one of the children interrupted her in a loud voice.

"Language."

A child with black eyes rose to his feet and asked in a provocative tone, "What's the use of language?"

"You'll read books."

"What's there in books?"

"All life's experiences."

"We don't want it."

The shouts of the young pupils went on repeating, "We don't want it."

Sternly Salma screamed, "Shut up."

"What do you want?" she enquired when the voices had quietened down.

"Sing to us."

"Dance."

"Talk to us about love."

One of them lit a cigarette and began blowing out the smoke with nervous irritation; another took a magazine from the drawer of the desk and engrossed himself in turning over the pages and gazing at the pictures of nude women.

A child with blond hair, a lock of which fell down over his

forehead, said, "I'm afraid of sleeping alone."

Salma smiled and asked gently, "What do you want of me?"

"Sleep with me."

"Won't your father object?" she enquired in a lively tone.

"He'll sleep with us."

Another student, smartly dressed, said, "Will you have dinner with me this evening?"

Salma gazed for a time at him without uttering a word.

One of the students waved about a knife with a shining blade and said to his companions, "I'll slaughter the neighbors' chickens, then I'll slaughter the neighbors' daughters, then I'll slaughter you." Suddenly two pupils stood up and began punching and slapping each other. The other pupils left their seats and gathered round the two of them, shouting fervently. Salma hurried toward the two children who were fighting and separated them. The other pupils, seizing the opportunity, began clutching hold of Salma and pinching her soft flesh with avid fingers. Salma did not get angry but laughed joyfully. "Why are you two quarreling?" she asked the two pupils.

"He asked me to tell him what my father does with my mother."

"Why didn't you tell him?" said Salma, feigning sorrow. "Don't you like to do good?" A hint of anger crept into her voice as she continued, "You must love others in order to be a good and complete human being. You are selfish. Do you love anyone?"

"I love our neighbor's wife."

"Why?"

"She's got a large and beautiful body."

"Would you love her if she were ugly?"

"No, I'd love her daughter."

At that moment the young children had all gathered round Salma, jostling in their eagerness to cling to her body.

The number of little hands that were touching her flesh increased. The softness of the flesh sent an evil spirit into the fingers, which were transformed into small ferocious animals.

Salma laughed joyfully. Her laughter was like a white raincloud passing across a blue summer sky. The children pushed and shoved one another all around her, like bees wanting to sip the nectar from a single flower.

As they touched the soft flesh the savagery of the fingers became more intense. The fingers tried to tear at the clothing. Salma resisted, laughing, but her feeble struggles were met with frenetic violence. She grew weak, her powers of resistance were eliminated and she was forced to yield and fall in exhaustion to the ground.

Salma was drowned in a flood of small hands that ripped apart all her clothing. She felt the tiled floor cold against her naked back, while the children, like numberless mysterious animals, pantingly crept across her flesh, squeezing it savagely.

Salma laughed as she almost attained the very heights of happiness, for in the past she had always hoped she would live with children who had not yet known the masks of the black earth. However, a frenzied sense of alarm suddenly seized her as the small teeth began gnawing her flesh and striking against solid bone.

The Ancient Gate

A blond soldier left the tavern with its clamor of drunken men. The mild eyes in their brown faces had taken on a glow of sullen hatred directly they had caught sight of him, for he was one of the foreign soldiers who had assaulted a city in which he had not been born.

He was enveloped by the silence of the street. At such a time it was empty, for when night neared its middle hour the city gave itself up to slumber, the lights in the windows were extinguished, and the alleys became deserted, the property of drunken strollers and gamblers returning home with weary steps.

The foreign soldier walked unsteadily by the river wall. The light breeze that brought the scent of jasmine, lemon blossom, and myrtle helped to clear his mind. The sound of gently rippling water filtered through in mournful complaint to his hearing.

Reaching the city's main square, he stopped for several moments, then set off down a side street. Implanted in the face of its stony surface were tramlines, with shops on either side, their iron doors barred. Lampposts stood at intervals casting a niggardly light.

The soldier carefully made his way between the tramlines. He imagined himself as a tram. He felt elated; he was a tram swaying slowly on its way. He remembered the days of his youth when, standing at the window of a train, he watched the green fields and villages give way to one another before his gaze. Now he was an express, an intoxicated tram, and the soldier started to run between the lines, his elation intensified. Imitating a tram, he let out a piercing tam, tam, tam. He continued to run until he tired. Panting, he came to a stop and looked about him. To his right was a dark lane, at the end of which shone a solitary lamp.

The foreign troops were warned against walking alone in the city's alleys.

The soldier sensed that a mysterious danger awaited him in the lane. An undefined longing to meet the danger, to challenge it, drove him on. He walked into the empty lane, singing in a harsh staccato voice till he reached the lamp. There stood one of the city's large gates, an ancient gate which had in olden times been closed at night to protect the city from its enemies.

The solider leaned against the gate, imagining he was hearing the clashing of swords, the neighing of horses, and voices raised in a repetition of "God is great."

All of a sudden he was seized by a strange fear. Hearing the fall of footsteps, he shivered in terrified anticipation and backed closer against the gate. A man and woman came into view conversing intimately as they walked. The woman was wearing a black head-wrap. The soldier was able to catch a glimpse of her face before, with a quick movement of her hand, she covered it over with a veil. It was a white and youthful face, shining alluringly through the darkness.

The foreign soldier's sense of loneliness increased and a feeling of unreasoning hatred exploded in him. Despite himself, he moved to block the way of the man and woman, possessed by an overwhelming desire to see the woman's unveiled face close to.

The woman let out a low cry of alarm. She placed herself

behind the man, grasping his waist, seeking his protection.

Like a blind man the soldier advanced, his hands held in front of him. He swayed and staggered in his attempts to grasp the woman, but the man fended him off, pushing him so violently in the chest that he reeled back. The woman set up a high-pitched wailing. The soldier, rooted to the spot, was paralyzed by fear. From far away he heard the sound of hurrying footsteps. Soon three men appeared wearing black baggy pants and red tarbooshes, who immediately grouped round the woman and her man.

"Don't be frightened, sister," one of them said to the woman. "Don't be frightened."

The four men stood poised in front of the soldier. A wonderful silence reigned; he was able to hear clearly the rumble of the river as it pursued its journey from one end of the city to the other.

Feeling threatened by a deadly danger, the soldier put his hand to his waist and tried to extract the revolver from its leather holster. The four men fell upon him and threw him to the ground. The soldier opened his mouth to call for help, but a dagger with a rigid blade struck at his neck. The cry was stifled and faded to a mumbling gasp

The four men took up the soldier's body and threw it into the dark river. The splash, like a cry for help, went unheard. Silence ruled for some moments, only to be put to flight by the sound of feet running away from the blood that soiled a patch of ground near the large and ancient gate.

In former days the gate had been part of a great stone wall encircling the city's houses and protecting them from enemies. Often the gate had been opened and men and horses and swords of steel had poured out through it. Now the walls had crumbled and nothing remained but scattered ruins, and the gate was ever open.

My Final Adventure

I walked about for a long time and when I was tired I went into a restaurant pretending to be looking for a friend. The tables were weighed down with plates of food, surrounded by mouths ever on the go.

I enquired of the waiter in a haughty voice, "Hasn't Mr. Amjad come yet?"

"Amjad?" said the waiter.

"Amjad al-Abbas," I said. "You must know him, he's a bank manager—he lunches with you every day."

The waiter hesitated. However, his hesitation lasted but a fleeting moment before it was transformed into a feeling of proud elation for the restaurant in which he worked and which bank managers frequented for lunch. "He hasn't come yet," he said. "He'll certainly be coming soon."

I looked at my wristwatch, saying, "No, no. Seeing that he hasn't come yet it must be that he's had to attend some urgent meeting."

I left the restaurant, dragging my feet, while saying to my

stomach severely, "Be careful not to utter a single word of discontent, for I never forced you to be my stomach."

"Have mercy on those on the earth and He who is in the heavens will have mercy on you," said my stomach.

At that instant I remembered the heavens which for days I had forgotten. I looked at them and they were clear and blue, and immediately I imagined to myself a woman with blue hair, green eyes, and black flesh, and with a red rose adorning her hair.

"How delicious grilled meat is!" shouted my stomach.

So I set about scolding it, soliciting it to be austere, and made my way to a small grocer's. The owner was an old man and I asked him to sell me two eggs, entreating him to choose two large-sized ones. As he took the price of them from me he said, "You'll have two eggs that are without comparison."

Then he added in a tone from which I was unable to judge whether he was being serious or sarcastic, "Shall I put them in a bag?"

"No . . . no . . . ." I said.

I took up the two eggs and placed one in my right pocket and the other in my left, and while I walked happily homewards I continued gently to touch them.

No sooner had I entered the house than I hurried to the kitchen and got out a plate. Taking an egg in each hand I struck them together, cracking one of them. There issued forth from it something that looked like a white chick. I said testily, "The shopkeeper has cheated me. I curse his forbearers, one by one."

I was rooted to the spot in astonishment when what I had imagined a chick began to grow until it became a man clothed in white and possessed of two wings. Seized with terror, I let the second egg slip from my hand, and it fell to the floor and broke. I looked at it sorrowfully, when from it too there emerged a white chick, which quickly grew and became, like its companion, a man with two wings. I put on a show of bravery and said, "What sort of a joke is this? Who are you?"

"I'm Munkar," said one of the men, and he pointed to his companion and said, "And this is Nakeer."

Then he added with boastful confidence, "No doubt you have heard a lot about us. We are the two angels who visit a dead man on the first night he spends in the grave and put him to account for what he did when he was alive."

"Why have you come to me?" I said. "I'm not dead and this house is not a grave; at the beginning of each month I pay to its owner a rent that takes up the greater part of my income."

Munkar and Nakeer exchanged looks of bewilderment and my annoyance increased. "Don't you believe I'm not dead?" I shouted at them. "If you don't believe it then I'll use my hand to persuade you otherwise."

"Don't be angry," said Munkar in an agitated voice. "What has happened is merely an accidental error. We apologize."

"We apologize sincerely," said Nakeer.

The two of them moved toward the kitchen door, so I stood in their way and asked irately, "Where are you off to?"

"There's a lot of work awaiting us," said Munkar.

"And the price of the two eggs that were spoiled, who's paying for that?"

Said Munkar, "We would like to make good the error but . . . "

"It's easy enough," I interrupted. "Pay me the price of the two eggs."

Raising his arms, Munkar said, "Search us. Our pockets are completely empty."

"Then I shall not let you go out," I said. "Should I remain foodless because of a mistake for which I was not responsible and had nothing to do with?"

"Be sensible," said Nakeer. "We've no money."

"But when we take you to account the day you die we shall overlook a not inconsiderable number of your sins."

I thought for a while, then said to them, "The word of men?"

They beat their wings as though in dissent and I hastened to say, "I mean, the word of angels?"

They nodded their heads smilingly, at which I moved away from the door and allowed them to leave.

I was no sooner alone than I was overcome with anger and the feeling that I had been cheated, so I said in a loud and threatening voice, "I'll curse the father of that cheating thief of a grocer. I'll go and bring down his shop about his head."

I left the house and hurried toward the old grocer's shop. As I reached it I found a large number of people gathered at the door staring down at the grocer, who was lying on the ground, motionless and with closed eyes.

"What's wrong with him?" I enquired of one of the spectators.

"The poor fellow was standing up and laughing and all of a sudden he fell to the ground and died."

I was disturbed and at a loss, not knowing what to do. After a while a white-colored ambulance came and stopped near the grocer's shop. The driver, accompanied by a nurse dressed in white, got down and, opening the back door of the ambulance, took out a stretcher. They shouted at the people to make way, and the people dispersed a bit. Then the driver and the nurse placed the stretcher on the ground and, chatting merrily, took up the grocer and threw him on to the stretcher and walked toward the ambulance. I rushed toward them shouting, for I remembered what had happened to me, "I'll not let you take him away."

"Be quiet," said the nurse. "There's no need to wail. If you're a relative of his, then go along with him."

With a swift movement they pushed the stretcher into the inside of the ambulance and got up into their places in the front of the vehicle. I found that there was nothing for it but to jump into the back of the ambulance.

The ambulance went off at speed, the horn's blaring making an easy path for it through the streets packed with people and cars.

I dug the old grocer in the ribs and said to him, "You cheat! You fraud! So you sell me rotten eggs? Aren't you ashamed of yourself?"

The grocer made no reply, so I said to him, "I know you're pretending to be dead so you can escape from me but you don't realize whose hands you've fallen into. You're unlucky. Listen here, I'll not let you go even if I have to go down into the grave with you. Pay me the price of the two eggs without any beating about the bush or else I'll pluck the hairs from your beard one by one."

At this the grocer opened his eyes and said to me angrily. "You really are a boy lacking in any sort of decent upbringing. Is this a way to talk to the dead? Death has a sanctity which much be observed."

"Go on with your preaching, go on," I said to him. "I'm not begging or asking for charity, I'm demanding my rights."

"Demand what you like," said the grocer. "Scream and tear your clothes. I'm dead, and if the driver and the nurse notice you're talking to me they'll take you off immediately to the lunatic asylum."

"I want my rights," I said, "and I shan't give them up, not if there were to be an earthquake."

The grocer closed his eyes. "Talk as you want," he said. "I'm dead and the dead don't talk."

I went on swearing at him for a long time but he paid me no attention. He remained silent, his flesh a yellowish color, and I was forced into silence when my voice grew hoarse.

I was aware of being about to choke, for the ambulance was narrow and its roof low and it was with difficulty that I breathed. I was amazed that the ambulance hadn't yet reached the hospital despite its having traveled such a long way.

I shouted at the driver and the nurse asking them to stop the ambulance but they paid no attention to me. The ambulance continued passing through street after street at full speed, so I opened the door, determined to throw myself out. But I didn't have the courage and after a while I found myself dragging the grocer off the stretcher. He put up no resistance and I flung him out of the ambulance, then laid myself down on the stretcher. I was conscious of the feelings of anger and exhaustion leaving me little by little, and it wasn't long before I gave myself up to sleep as the ambulance went on rushing through the streets, expelling a continuous wailing from its horn.

When, after a time, I woke up, I was surprised to find myself in a dark place. I attempted in vain to stand up.

Suddenly there flashed out a bright beam of an electric light directed toward me, and I heard a mocking voice addressing me, "So here we are, we've soon met up."

It seemed to me I'd heard that voice before. Then I heard a second voice saying, "We've been granted a great opportunity to give him a welcome that will make him forget his mother."

My astonishment increased, for the second voice too I had heard previously.

"It appears he's got a weak memory and has forgotten us."

I heard footsteps and the owners of the two voices approached.

I found that they were Munkar and Nakeer. They carried whips, their clothes were black, and their eyes stern and cruel.

I wanted to speak but couldn't.

"Do you know what we are going to do to you?" said Munkar. "We shall go on beating you till we tear your flesh into tiny pieces where worms will live and eat you up slowly, and rats will come and swallow what remains."

I tried to speak, to remind them of their promise, but I was not able to. They noticed my attempt and laughed gleefully. Munkar brought his clenched hand up to the light from the lamp; when he opened it there hung down a piece of flesh that dripped blood. "Do you know what this is?" he said to me. "It's your tongue and we've cut it off so you won't chatter and give us a headache."

Closing my eyes, I embedded my nails in the ground. My strangled calls for help grew louder and louder but Munkar and Nakeer paid me no attention. They presented me with many papers saying, "These papers are written in your hand and comprise your admission of the sins you've committed, so come along and sign them or else . . . "

Without any hesitation at all I hastened to sign them and awaited in terror for the whips. But suddenly the lamp was put out and silence reigned, and when my eyes got used to the darkness I discovered that Munkar and Nakeer had disappeared. I was delighted, but after a while I felt so lonely I burst into loud weeping. Then I was forced into silence, embarrassed by the grumbling voices I heard demanding their right to peace and quiet after death.

After some days a hungry rat visited me and we agreed together that he would eat my right leg and in exchange bring me a transistor radio.

The rat honored the agreement and I was able to listen to songs and news bulleting while the rate ate my leg at leisure, licking his lips with joy and telling me from time to time that he hadn't broken his promise.

After several more days I began to think about a second deal by which I would give up my left leg in exchange for a small television set.

Modern Arabic Literature
from the American University in Cairo Press

Ibrahim Abdel Meguid *Birds of Amber* • *Distant Train*
No One Sleeps in Alexandria • *The Other Place*
Yahya Taher Abdullah *The Collar and the Bracelet*
The Mountain of Green Tea
Leila Abouzeid *The Last Chapter*
Hamdi Abu Golayyel *Thieves in Retirement*
Yusuf Abu Rayya *Wedding Night*
Ahmed Alaidy *Being Abbas el Abd*
Idris Ali *Dongola* • *Poor*
Radwa Ashour *Granada*
Ibrahim Aslan *The Heron* • *Nile Sparrows*
Alaa Al Aswany *Chicago* • *Friendly Fire* • *The Yacoubian Building*
Fadhil al-Azzawi *Cell Block Five* • *The Last of the Angels*
Liana Badr *The Eye of the Mirror*
Hala El Badry *A Certain Woman* • *Muntaha*
Salwa Bakr *The Golden Chariot* • *The Man from Bashmour*
The Wiles of Men
Halim Barakat *The Crane*
Hoda Barakat *Disciples of Passion* • *The Tiller of Waters*
Mourid Barghouti *I Saw Ramallah*
Mohamed Berrada *Like a Summer Never to Be Repeated*
Mohamed El-Bisatie *Clamor of the Lake*
Houses Behind the Trees • *Hunger*
A Last Glass of Tea • *Over the Bridge*
Mahmoud Darwish *The Butterfly's Burden*
Tarek Eltayeb *Cities without Palms*
Mansoura Ez Eldin *Maryam's Maze*
Ibrahim Farghali *The Smiles of the Saints*
Hamdy el-Gazzar *Black Magic*
Tawfiq al-Hakim *The Essential Tawfiq al-Hakim*
Abdelilah Hamdouchi *The Final Bet*
Fathy Ghanem *The Man Who Lost His Shadow*
Randa Ghazy *Dreaming of Palestine*
Gamal al-Ghitani *Pyramid Texts* • *The Zafarani Files* • *Zayni Barakat*
Yahya Hakki *The Lamp of Umm Hashim*
Bensalem Himmich *The Polymath* • *The Theocrat*
Taha Hussein *The Days* • *A Man of Letters* • *The Sufferers*
Sonallah Ibrahim *Cairo: From Edge to Edge* • *The Committee* • *Zaat*
Yusuf Idris *City of Love and Ashes* • *The Essential Yusuf Idris*
Denys Johnson-Davies *The AUC Press Book of Modern Arabic Literature*
In a Fertile Desert: Modern Writing from the United Arab Emirates
Under the Naked Sky: Short Stories from the Arab World

Said al-Kafrawi *The Hill of Gypsies*
Sahar Khalifeh *The End of Spring*
The Image, the Icon, and the Covenant • *The Inheritance*
Edwar al-Kharrat *Rama and the Dragon* • *Stones of Bobello*
Betool Khedairi *Absent*
Mohammed Khudayyir *Basrayatha*
Ibrahim al-Koni *Anubis* • *Gold Dust* • *The Seven Veils of Seth*
Naguib Mahfouz *Adrift on the Nile* • *Akhenaten: Dweller in Truth*
Arabian Nights and Days • *Autumn Quail* • *The Beggar*
The Beginning and the End • *Cairo Modern*
The Cairo Trilogy: Palace Walk, Palace of Desire, Sugar Street
Children of the Alley • *The Day the Leader Was Killed*
The Dreams • *Dreams of Departure* • *Echoes of an Autobiography*
The Harafish • *The Journey of Ibn Fattouma* • *Karnak Café*
Khan al-Khalili • *Khufu's Wisdom* • *Life's Wisdom* • *Midaq Alley*
The Mirage • *Miramar* • *Mirrors* • *Morning and Evening Talk*
Naguib Mahfouz at Sidi Gaber • *Respected Sir* • *Rhadopis of Nubia*
The Search • *The Seventh Heaven* • *Thebes at War*
The Thief and the Dogs • *The Time and the Place*
Voices from the Other World • *Wedding Song*
Mohamed Makhzangi *Memories of a Meltdown*
Alia Mamdouh *The Loved Ones* • *Naphtalene*
Selim Matar *The Woman of the Flask*
Ibrahim al-Mazini *Ten Again*
Yousef Al-Mohaimeed *Wolves of the Crescent Moon*
Ahlam Mosteghanemi *Chaos of the Senses* • *Memory in the Flesh*
Mohamed Mustagab *Tales from Dayrut*
Buthaina Al Nasiri *Final Night*
Ibrahim Nasrallah *Inside the Night*
Haggag Hassan Oddoul *Nights of Musk*
Mohamed Mansi Qandil *Moon over Samarqand*
Abd al-Hakim Qasim *Rites of Assent*
Somaya Ramadan *Leaves of Narcissus*
Lenin El-Ramly *In Plain Arabic*
Ghada Samman *The Night of the First Billion*
Rafik Schami *Damascus Nights* • *The Dark Side of Love*
Khairy Shalaby *The Lodging House*
Miral al-Tahawy *Blue Aubergine* • *Gazelle Tracks* • *The Tent*
Bahaa Taher *As Doha Said* • *Love in Exile*
Fuad al-Takarli *The Long Way Back*
Zakaria Tamer *The Hedgehog*
M.M. Tawfik *Murder in the Tower of Happiness*
Mahmoud Al-Wardani *Heads Ripe for Plucking*
Latifa al-Zayyat *The Open Door*